Kerana Angelova

ELADA PINYO and TIME

Kerana Angelova

and

novel

Translated by

Hristina Keranova

Accents Publishing and Publishing House SIGNS
Lexington, Kentucky • Burgas, Bulgaria • 2016

Printed in the United States of America

Accents Publishing
Translator: Hristina Keranova
Cover Artist: Nevena Angelova

Library of Congress Control Number: 2016946845
ISBN: 978-1-936628-43-8
First Edition

This book has been translated with financial support from the National Culture Fund in Bulgaria.

Accents Publishing is an independent press for brilliant voices. For a catalog of current and upcoming titles, please visit us on the Web at

www.accents-publishing.com

~ *CONTENTS* ~

~ *PROLOGUE* ~

Under the weight of her years, she felt like an old quince tree. The fruit has long been picked, but the weary branches sag as if it still carried the load. "My time has come," muttered old Pinyo. One evening something squeaked pitifully in her chest and she imagined a newly-hatched, naked bird fluttering in her rib cage. Probably eaglet, ravenous, and I have to feed him with my flesh. Still thinking about it, she saw in a flash how time flipped into a headfirst position in the womb of eternity, its forehead forward again. Where to though? And who gave her the eyes to see this? She smiled and waved her hand. Her life was already flowing backwards and the questions did not need answers.

As she was flying headlong backwards, she suspected that death would be a lot like life. At least as singular and unique. The eaglet pecked at her ribs, tore a painful piece of her flesh. The pain brought a revelation: her one and only death turned out to be a return. The strangest thing about it was that she could see her whole life at once. It was as if I was traveling by train, leaning comfortably against the plush back of the seat, only I was traveling in the opposite direction. Behind the windows trees flow smoothly, clouds, haymakers, fiery horses stretching their necks into sunsets, bridges, train stations, birds, dogs, people. Here I am, sitting and watching, when out of the blue, the future pops up from behind my back and before my very eyes turns into the past. And my reflection in the window shows a woman with violet eyes getting younger and younger, turning into a girl with wild, raven black hair, and then into a child.

With that thought she arrived.

The house still stood at the top of the steep street, as she faintly remembered, only it was gray from the bitter winds of time. Dark brown salt crystals stuck to the walls and the beams under the roof, green with mold. The cap of ash on top of the chimney was like a soft nest. A bare baby bird lay in the nest, rolled its only yellow eye and clucked unkindly: cluck, cluck, cluck!

The smell of freshly-baked bread wafted from the fields. Up the steep slope rolled a ruddy loaf of cornbread and to her amazement, ducked into the backyard. Yeah, figured Pinyo, it's rushing to make a lap of its field first, and soon granny will break a hot chunk from it and slip it into my hands. She sighed. How did she think of all this? That was not the childhood she had, here or elsewhere. Could I be cheating? Could I be trying to live a better life now? Could it be that this time the others would not mess up my life either? Oh God, what would I do without my life's mistakes! She smiled bitterly.

At the same time, she was becoming aware of the forgotten feeling of childhood, those strange butterflies in the stomach. A blue bug flew out of a rose bush, landed plump on her palm, crawled softly. Her lips swelled from the sensuous nectar of its touch, the sky lit up, she felt as if she owned the world. She had no memories, they were still in the future, they had not returned yet. Creak, creak, the gate happily creaked with Pinyo swaying, one foot on it. The past happens so fast, I've become so little, she thought.

Suddenly it was dark. Dark always came as a surprise.

Her joy died. In the nearby gully jackals howled; her blood curdled. Only then did she realize that the village was deserted—not a sound, not a breath. Mom! Mother! Her mother's image rose in the windows of the house, a halo of light around her head from the gas lamp. She was young and thoughtful. She reached her hand out of the kitchen window and placed it on the child's head, on the pulsating fontanel. The jackals sang again. "Don't worry," her mother smiled, "it's the crickets, remember? See how big and warm the night is, bad things won't happen to you."

Her duck legs wobbled as Pinyo tried to reach her mother. She clung to her, buried her face in her lap. Cooed. The mother laid her head on a folded elbow and nursed her yet for another first time. Pinyo choked with the warm gulps, waved her hands and legs, and stared at the golden eye of the bare-necked baby bird, perched on the windowsill. The eye was getting even bigger and more golden. I've never thought that light springs from the eye of an ugly, bald baby bird, wondered Pinyo as her last breath was leaving her.

She strained to grasp the main reason, the sole reason that made her come way back in time to its entrance, which was also the exit. She couldn't, though. There was no reply. It seemed that man was a hoax, from the very start, to the end. Lord, how absurd man is! A cry of desperation surged to her lips and a mighty voice suddenly rang out:

"Pinyo, somewhere along the tangled course of time, in an instant of the present, past or future, the answer will find you itself!"

She sighed with relief.

At that moment the eye of the ugly bird turned into a dazzling golden sun.

PART ONE

DEEP DOWN IN THE BACKWOODS THE PAST WILL HAPPEN TOMORROW

Deep down in the backwoods, it was desolate and magnificent. *Farewell, forgive me, I can't.* Mother untied her scarlet apron, made it into a swinging cradle, tied it to a lower branch. *I can't, forgive me, I don't want to.* In a quiet trance, she repeated again and again a monotonous song without a melody. A scrawny old man stood beside her sniffing and shaking all over. "It's time," his shrill voice rose, and Mother turned green with terror. She rolled her eyes, threw her hands straight up and froze. "Save the others, go save them," the old man whined. He started pummeling her with his fists, harder and harder to get her out of the trance. At last, she dropped her hands, grabbed her head, closed her eyelids tight and rushed blindly through the woods. She bounced off the trunks of trees, first inadvertently, then with all her might. The old man staggered after her, stumbled and shook his head. They were hoping to catch up with the other refugees.

I was left alone, wild with terror.

Days and nights passed. The nappy clinging to my body felt too tight; chills, like ants, crawled up my hands and legs; from the long lying on my back, my neck was red and painful. I was ravenously hungry. At night I could see the lights in the wood: bluish radiance rose from the rotten hollows in some trees, the eyes of the night birds shone high in the branches.

One early evening an old man with a long milky-white beard came down the hill across, an owl clinging to his shoulder. What brought him here out of nowhere, his body all chlorophyll and light as if a walking tree among the trees? He crossed the meadow, his cloak soaked the dew and turned black. He bent over the cradle, his pale white irises pierced through me and somehow, I guessed his thought, *I'm not your fate, your fate is called Hrisoula.* To my consternation, ignoring my screams of protest, he walked straight through the bushes and vanished into the dawn like a shadow. A man came and was gone. Loneliness was so scary that I had to admit its presence as I lay in my cradle watching the sky, in the grips of infinite, cosmic loneliness.

A baby in the cradle sensing the approaching death, oh Lord, we don't always understand your divine scheme!

However, this sense of infinity did not surprise me, my perceptions were powerful, crystal clear and complete. I looked down and saw my own cradle with the flaccid little body in it. Poor, wrinkled, abandoned body which I pitied with all the pity in the world. I was flying higher and higher, amazed and happily desperate, I discovered how widely I spread over the Strandja mountain when I saw all its paths at once, twisting and writhing like moon snakes. Here and there white springs glowed, in the indigo darkness the eyes of hiding jackals flashed like embers, in the deep grass the antlers of the sleeping deer glowed like royal crowns.

I could see it all at once though the eyes of the bruised, flaccid body in the cradle were closed tightly in complete blindness. I did not know then that the soul sees without eyes; it was not possible to know this in the unconscious age when only the senses are so vital, but make no mistake, my soul could see.

Everything lasted just an instant. I was again aware only of myself: I was hungry, thirsty and alive. I squirmed with colic, whimpered, rebelled against the narrowness of the cradle, and exhausted, fell asleep at last. Then the mighty, comforting presence of something streaming from all directions rocked me—when I opened my eyes after a while, it was still around, everywhere,

The Great Cosmic Maternal Instinct.

I felt caressed. From all directions. Yet, I was faint with hunger and groaned. Tilting my head backwards, I saw mom's bright eyes. I was not surprised at all. When she bent over me, I breathed in the familiar smell of milk and bit hard into the firm teat seeking my face. I sucked greedily, choking, and drops trickled down my cheeks … When I was full and belched contentedly, the sky had already begun to brighten, the flickering light made me squint my eyes. Through my half-closed eyelids, I looked at mom and saw that she was a doe, big, gray and calm. She was looking at me with human eyes and I smiled back at her.

The old woman's mind is clear, her memory strong and her vocabulary rich. Her style of expression is quite unique and comes alive with sudden archaisms and dialect words—on the generally elegant verbal background, they are bright and unexpected and attract attention like glass beads sparkling occasionally in a pearl necklace. At times Elada Pinyo behaves like a sophisticated French woman: her gestures, the gentle finesse of her little finger away from the others, her bright suits, lace handkerchiefs, silk white socks, her hats ... And then lo and behold, she'd perk up, suddenly gesticulating like a peasant woman; she'd roll her eyes, put defiant little fists on her waist, and looking like the Bulgarian letter Ф, she would storm into her mother tongue, rounding even more the round Strandja vowels, "Gee, a hundred year old hag, that's me, but look, I'm still not a good-for-nothing!"

Good for nothing ... Like her Bulgarian sometimes, a language peculiar, colorful, figurative, but as if translated in her mind in a flash from another, unfamiliar, only her own, existing nowhere in the world. The reason is that our language is who we are, our one and only life, our deep unspoken essence that we call the Word of God in us, and we are too humble to express it fully, but the old woman is quick to speak her essence, impatient; she's rushing to get somewhere and all of us around gasp when we breathe in the same air and we hurry to catch up with her.

She befriended us a few years ago when that rascal son of mine started to greet the French teacher at school with "Don Juan, Madame Taneva"; terrified, Madame recommended a tutor with a Parisian accent, we invited her to educate our smart alec, and this extraordinary old woman arrived in our home, appeared devotedly on the doorstep, as if she were a gift from someone who knew what we needed most in this life. "Bonjour, Madame Elada," the youngster would greet her sullenly in those early days, apparently more in favor of his own greeting, but his French improved so much that one day our Madame with glowing eyes presented him with a French book, its pages yellowed with time.

"It's for you, from Syruie."

"Who is Syruie?" we asked in unison.

"Do not rush," said the old woman, "Syruie is something

so beautiful and unattainable that you shouldn't rush to get to know her."

A routine lesson begins; she's dark and thin, with hair like a silver spider web on her balding head, eyes like purple pansies on her weather-beaten face, feet like thin sticks clad in white socks even in summer, fingers so thin that the rays of light piercing their tips makes them transparent, and so sudden she is every time, so not-from-here and close to my soul as if I had created her not to be lonely in this life,

when I touch her arm,

she smiles,

"What if it's me smiling to myself from some other time, some other space?

Let's drink tea on the terrace ..."

We sit on the terrace and watch the bustling Bogoridi. The boulevard flows by, a motley human stream: girls in pink shorts like large butterflies, guys on roller skates, mothers pushing strollers with babies inside kicking the air with plump little legs, by gosh, I was exactly like them a century ago ... the jukebox blares heavy metal in the cafe across; among the bright graffiti on its walls, a greeting in red letters says, hello, millennium, goodbye, millennium; it's been there for two years as a reminder of the human delusion that time can be defined and categorized ... The old woman, however, has stopped watching the commotion, her bottomless violet eyes come closer and she whispers confidentially, "I remember my whole life up to this very minute!"

"So do I. We all remember our lives, Elada Pinyo."

"I'm telling you something else. I remember every second of my life. I mean that if I start telling you my life's story, it will take me another hundred years."

"That's not possible at all. If so, you have a leak in your

subconscious, or how come your mind did not explode with so much information?"

"It's a gift I have."

"I've never heard of such a gift. What are you talking about! Can one remember all the millions of seconds in a life—both what's necessary, and what's not? Surely, your life's had its share of the terrible and unbearable."

"We call life unbearable and yet we bear it. Remember, in life you don't get what you don't need. Turn on the TV, will you?"

"Female Presence" is on, with Romy Schneider and Yves Montand. We set up to watch inside, and we quietly sink into the human drama, feeling like one in the shared silence. "Misery must be respected and one must learn to curse," says the man in the movie. "If I'm ever happy, I'll seek a cure," the woman replies.

The same sadness covers the faces of Romy, Yves Montand, my old lady. It's the face of suffering, tinged with the shadow of something else—cathartic, fleeting. What could be more than suffering or happiness?

The man in the movie says, "You think you howl out of loneliness, not knowing that it's love."

Elada stirs next to me as if waking from a narcotic state. "He said the same!" She lifts her head and looks straight into my eyes, guessing my thought in some mysterious way,

"Suffering is bigger than happiness and happiness and suffering are bigger than suffering, especially if they visit us together. If you haven't experienced this, you will sooner or later and you have to be ready to face both—don't turn your head away, be brave when you meet them because together they are something else."

Suddenly she changes the topic,

"I want to tell you about my life because I have four more months to go, just enough to tell you the most important. I have jotted down some notes, two notebooks, they'll will be my gift to you."

"How come you're so sure you have only four months?!"

She laughs heartily,

"You say only four months, I said four months more. My time and your time do not run the same, mon cher, but we have four whole months at our disposal!"

We start as soon as the next day. Elada tells what she hasn't told in the notebooks, and I take notes but mostly, I listen entranced and time starts to return. This went on for four months …

One morning she did not show up at my place. We found her on the terrace in her home, sunk in a wicker chair, with her hands on her left chest, as if she was holding a newly-hatched bird. Two notebooks lay on her knees, the same title on the covers "The Past Will Happen Tomorrow."

So here I am, trying to tell the old woman Elada Pinyo, tell about myself through her, tell about heaven and earth within us; I try to find the words to match the intelligence of her written speech, her gift of a true storyteller; however, I need the words to find me the way they found her, the words to reveal our mysterious nature, to share about our extraordinary closeness, to tell about her astounding life, so we are one here, and beyond,

and we don't howl at the sky out of loneliness, not knowing it's love.

All through the week the doe came at dawn. After offering me her teat, she waited patiently until I was full and then I screamed in delight, but the pain in the nape of my neck kept gnawing at me and I cried, my mouth gaping. My nappy was soaked with urine and the feces covered me up to my shoulders. The doe smelled my wretchedness and stepped under the cradle. She propped it up with her back and I thumped on the ground with my face in the grass. I felt the animal's rough tongue on the back of my neck: she was gently licking the salty wound; blissful, I stopped crying, and my wide open nostrils breathed in the smell of wet earth. Lustrous acorns sparkled in the underbrush, wild pears and serviceberries rotted and mushy fruit smelled sweet; hedgehogs lifted their snouts to sniff the autumn air, mushrooms, shriveled crab apples and leaves stuck on their needles. The doe kept licking the wound with its healing tongue, then she bit the swaddling and chewed it until it snapped. I felt relieved as if the devil's claws had let me go and my purple body sighed with all its pores. The fetid nappies peeled off, the rags got caught in the bushes and waved from the twigs while my body continued to roll, naked and free. It stopped at the trunk of a tree. The morning frost had washed the dirt, my skin glowed, clean and fresh. Freedom is always more than we can bear, so it overwhelmed me and exhausted, I fell asleep at the tree.

When I awoke, I was in a cradle. I felt a warm blanket on top—I was buried, a pile of leaves covered me. I peeked out and looked around. I thought I saw the old man with the owl, peering from behind a tree and when our glances met, he vanished in a second in the morning mist, just melted away.

Although it's the end of October, a pink blossom is opening right by me, a low thick sweet briar. Its pale colors sparkle in the sun, just above the cradle. I sit up, reach out with my hand, carefully pick off a slender leaf, chew it with my sharp front teeth and squint with pleasure. It's been another week of life away from people and close to the beasts, reptiles and birds: I drink the dew, suck from the doe's teats and silently repeat the words of my mother tongue *bread, Elada, house, sky, milk, hollyhock, water, mom's little beetle, the blue one,* not fully understanding their meaning, I feel that I should remember them, that I need them like life and death; *forgive me, farewell, I can't,* all of them surge inside me and then I just laugh or cry, thus expressing their intimate, profound meaning.

I suspect that the doe's milk was not the only thing that saved me at this point in my life; I suspect that what saved me were those deeply cherished words, whose meaning cannot be expressed. The truth is that it was then that I developed my unique gift to guess the meaning of the words by their aura and memorize every second of my life; as my memory and life grew more condensed, the sweet briar responded to my cries and laughter by closing its petals in fear or spreading the pink silk of its soul with tenderness and trust.

One afternoon, when the sun shoots its fragile spears through the thick branches, I hear crackling of twigs behind my back: many feet thumping, loud voices shouting at each other. Excited, I lift my head and look around, but I don't see a soul and the clamor dies away. I'm about to scream in despair when a husky female voice gasps happily, just a step away from my cradle.

Never again in my life would I meet such a lovely girl. Tall and slim, with wavy tendrils of raven hair, she stood at the bush, clapped her hands in admiration of the wild roses, spoke in her own strange language, replete in soft and frequent sibilants, and her slightly husky voice had something so lovely in it! I laugh through my tears but the girl does not hear; she starts picking the pale petals off to hide them in her bosom, and after rubbing the olive skin of her face with the last one, she walks away to catch up with the others.

Then I somehow sensed that I should keep quiet and just stare at the nape of her neck. I did not understand why, but I watched without blinking, my pupils huge, my eyelids stuck wide open. As she was scurrying down the path, the girl froze in her steps and waited as if remembering something, then she turned abruptly and our eyes met.

I could have done the easier thing—cry loudly or scream, but instead kept quiet. I hushed and froze in my cradle and waited. Maybe because if your destiny gets in your way and it is really yours, not somebody else's, it will see you even with her back.

"Hrisoula!" somebody shouted from afar, so my destiny's name was in truth Hrisoula. The girl did not reply; with trembling hands, she searched through the dry leaves, dug me out of the cradle, rolled her bright green eyes and since she was used to clapping her hands when surprised, she laid me at her feet, clapped, but came to her senses, grabbed me again and started to yell in her husky language.

They wondered and rejoiced and then put me up in a big luggage basket. The basket had a twin sister—Hrisoula's kittens traveled in it. They had tied the baskets together and flung them on the back of a bony donkey. We wobbled on its back along hardly visible paths, about twenty Karakachan women, two men with two mules and the donkey; children too, babies in cheesecloth bags, hanging from the backs of the women. The Karakachan women were going back home from the cabins in Bulgaria to the cabins in Edirne, before the men and the flocks.

Settled in my basket, I was balancing somehow and looking at the wide world. Hrisoula would come see me every now and then, poke the dimple on my chin with her finger, chattering fast in her low husky voice and the scent of wild roses and care would waft from her bosom. She'd sometimes sigh and shake her head like an old woman: "Hey, you, lost Bulgarian." I tried quite successfully to imitate Hrisoula's raspy words, rustling like dry leaves. They had guessed that I was a child of Bulgarians by my mother's scarlet woven apron and they suspected that the whirlwind of the Bulgarian uprising called *Preobrazhenie* had blown the parents far away, leaving the child in God's hands. Because I could not walk yet, sometimes Hrisoula would take me in her arms, so I wouldn't get stiff in the basket and she'd chatter non-stop, laugh, sometimes cry and look at me sympathetically, with eyes washed in her tears.

Gradually, I got to know her and grew fatefully attached to her. The young Karakachan woman was willful and painfully independent, very much unlike the others, except for the language. The women in the group wore tiaras of twisted kerchiefs on their heads even in the hottest days, but Hrisoula walked bareheaded, her hair tousled by the thorny bushes, a blue loose end headscarf fluttering on her neck. The others had two or three black skirts on, spread out like the wings of butterflies, but heavy and cumbersome, while Hrisoula was running around in a short woven hemp shirt, well above the ankles. Like all the other women, she had soft shoes on. She'd pick arguments with her companions several times a day, mainly with her sister Katerina.

A stout woman with a milky white face, as most Karakachan women, Katerina carries a cheesecloth bag on her back with a round-faced, pink-cheeked baby peeking from it, and walks in silence with large, manly strides. While Hrisoula talks excitedly with everything around—me in the basket or the crocuses in the bushes, the birds in the sky and whatever else she wants, Katerina is silent and calm; only rarely she'd utter a muffled, heavy word in a defiantly nonchalant manner, looking down at her feet, as they were cracking dry twigs on her path; then Hrisoula's temper flares up even more, she snaps off the first twig crossing her way and whips her bare ankles with it, agitated and angry.

Her love outbursts were not less passionate—she hugged the kittens tightly in her arms, they meowed loudly in protest and scratched her in defense, and her hands were scarred by their wild claws; she hurriedly stole kisses on their throats and her laugh rang; when she got tired of the kittens, she came to the basket to play with me. She tickled me sometimes and I giggled madly, but then the women indignantly reminded her that tickling could be deadly, and she'd poke the dimple on my chin, open my mouth to see how I was teething, or thrust in my ears soft rags, wrapped around a stick. She smelled of roses and wild mint—her bosom was filled with their fine leaves and every day she changed them to keep the smell fresh. One day it occurred to her to fill the basket with geranium and mint—she piled them on top of me up to the mouth; their fragrance made me dizzy, I felt I was losing consciousness, and it was so nice, I could die of happiness; and that's how it was later in my life: somehow I found the strength to survive the worst that often popped up out of the blue, but when the good in my life was too much, it overwhelmed me, took my strength and I could just lie there and die, blissful and ravished, unless a subconscious thought stopped me with the realization that the moment will be as short-lived as a child's sigh. Then I'd collect myself and muster my courage to survive the happiness.

One day Hrisoula stopped in her tracks and startled the others with her cry, "Stop right now, stop, I'm telling you, my baby has no name! I just thought of a name, she'll be Despina, Pina for short, I'll call her Pinyo." The others had no objections and Hrisoula started calling me Pinyo right away.

One evening we reached the end of the mountain; down at the foothills, the field was as flat as a baking pan. From here to the cabins, the walk would last from sunrise to sunset, so we had almost reached home; the Karakachan women started chattering excitedly, lit fires, nursed the babies and took out the sleeping mats.

Dusk was falling when the doe appeared. She was not

just coming, she was swimming in the gray air fluttering playfully around her. They all saw her because she was not hiding; they screamed, rushed to chase her and I shouted loudly, but she darted faster than the wind, her skin flashing in the ivy thickets across; "Me-me-me," the kids chanted to lure her, their voices echoing through the silence of the evening woods—when dusk is falling, the woods stand still and quiet in a peculiar way, time stops there and nothing is what it was. Indeed, time in the mountain runs only when people move through it, then they call their own movement time. Now the flux of magnificent calm coming from all directions was shattered by the clamor of human voices.

The doe finally turned away and reluctantly headed towards the heart of the night, only her oval mirror showed white in the dark and the crack of twigs under her feet echoed. When she melted in the dark, I stopped screaming, all other children calmed down too, and soon all stretched on the mats and fell asleep.

In the morning we started early, went down to the flat valley and were soon on our way. Hrisoula looked back after a while and I followed her glance—the mountain was waking up too; low haze was rising up its ridges, the treetops were ablaze, warmed by the fire of the rising sun. At the end of the wood, at the very end, the doe stood and looked after us. On impulse, Hrisoula's hand covered her mouth. I turned over in my basket and flopped on my belly.

"Pinyo-oh," echoes Hrisoula's desperate cry, her hands on her waist. The sunset spreads its generous rays through the branches of the old trees and the girl is all a-glow. She had probably slept in the shadow of a tree and yawning sweetly, she stretches and puts her hands on her waist again. Her eyes search the thickets, and after a while, she snaps, fear in her voice, "I'll count to three and if you don't show up right now, Pinyo, you no longer live in my hut, is that clear? There!" She spits and her saliva sparkles in the grass like a snail trail. She searches for me randomly, shouting to high heaven all the time.

I keep quiet, hiding in the hollow of an ancient tree.

I grew up, imperceptibly—I'm about five now, my hair reaches to my waist and I am very proud that it is black and glossy like Hrisoula's; my eyes are like hers, so the others say. Hrisoula fakes anger, "Well, well so much beauty is not a good thing; I can't look you in the eyes, they blind me with all that blue sky in them, and on top of all your skin has a dark tinge like mine; that's enough shame, Pinyo!" I am angrier than her, I knock my fists together, "It's you blind me, your goggles are like the sea, the White one, so there!"

I've already seen the sea, not only one, but two, the Black and the White, each bluer than the other. The Karakachans have cabins in Greece, in Bulgaria, and in Edirne and move from one place to another, changing the grazing grounds for the sheep. They are excellent sheep breeders, the best on the Balkans; their sheep have fleeces like black clouds and their udders touch the ground. The Karakachan shepherds know where the lushest grass grows and lead their flocks there.

Now we are in the mountains above Sliven. The sky's blue is so deep that looking up, you feel something hurts in your chest; transparent cobwebs fill the air, and though it is still summer, the scent of fall is everywhere. The herds are out grazing and all men are with them. The women boil and curdle the milk to make cheese, wash the cans, cook and bake bread. As twilight descends, a man on a mule comes down from the pasture, the cans rattle, the milk still steaming inside smells sweet. Hrisoula's cats smell it first and start meowing wildly. And I, Pinyo, start shaking all over.

"That wretched Pinyo has lived with these people for so many years, yet every day she laps milk straight from the copper pots and she never gets tired of it!" When I first saw the bursting udders of the sheep, I staggered with ecstasy. I remembered the doe and her warm teat, I could not forget how they saved me from death. When you come to know death too early, you get so jealously attached to life, greedily clinging to its teats.

First they tried to feed me from a bottle full of fresh milk with a twisted cheesecloth around its neck to suck from. I pushed it away in disgust and turned my head. When they gave up on me, I crawled out of the basket to the sheep, always grazing around the camp. I lay under the nearest one, grabbed the udder and sucked, choking in the rush, afraid somebody could see me. But once, Hrisoula saw, yelled and even spanked my skinny ass. Even though she was always on the alert, I often stalked past her, crawled to the sheep and sucked wildly, with delight, until the sharp eyes of a Karakachan woman caught sight of me. Then Hrisoula slapped her thighs in amazement, raised her hands to the sky and spoke hurriedly, even rolled her eyes to make me understand what a bad thing I'd done, but I could neither explain nor could they understand how much I needed the warmth of the doe. Then Hrisoula thrust the bottle in my hands and I sucked under her watchful gaze. That's how I was growing up.

Now Hrisoula is searching the woods for me, but I sit in the tree hollow and I am happy—I smell the wood, the wild honey, bees are probably nearby; Hrisoula's Pinyo-oh fades in the distance and so what if this time I don't get away with the spanking, so grand are the mountains, so majestic!

Yet, I crawl out of the tree hollow and amble around looking for Hrisoula. Dusk is falling. As if from under the earth's surface, the voices of women and children come to me from the spring in the gully. I can't hear Hrisoula's voice, she is quiet, and I feel a little disoriented, but I catch sight of a freshly broken twig where a path starts, aha-aa, I am heading there to see what my eyes would never forget.

Hrisoula stands at the end of the path and talks to Katerina's husband, Yorgos. Gesticulating excitedly in his face, she explains something in her usual way. Yorgos listens eagerly, the loaded mules behind him, the cans rattling from time to time. I was about to dash to join them when the man impulsively grips the girl's thin arm, Hrisoula shuts up and pulls a step back. The man grabs her other arm. He utters something and buries his face in her shoulder. They stand still. So do I, but my heart is pounding wildly. Hrisoula breaks out of her daze, pulls back a little, props her hands on Yorgos' chest and pushes him away. Then she turns around abruptly and runs down the path. I hardly manage to hide behind a nearby tree when she rushes past me, her cheeks burning, her hair flying. Yorgos doesn't budge.

I watch him anxiously. Yorgos is a big man, with broad shoulders and hairy chest, face covered in thick red beard, and shoulder-length hair, even more golden than his beard. He is quieter than his wife Katerina, and we often see him sitting still on the rock in front of the hut, his big brown eyes staring at the sunset. Heavy, uncouth, secretive, he scares me.

Yorgos finally leaves, the obedient mules hauling the white milk cans after him. He passes by me, but does not see me. I sneak behind him and when we arrive, I slip into our hut. Hrisoula crouches on the straw mat on the floor, her face buried in her knees. I play around with the kittens, but she chases us away, "Off with you, leave me alone!"

Days pass, and again I happen to see Hrisoula with Yorgos and everything is repeated. One day I spotted her behind a low tree watching something with squinted eyes. I look that way too.

In front of their hut Katerina helps Yorgos wash: scoops water with the wooden ladle, pours it over the man's head, lathers his hair with soapwort and then rubs it with her fingers. He is kneeling, she has his back between her strong thighs, she's taken off the heavy skirts and her body sways rhythmically, white and ripe.

Katerina rinses Yorgos' hair, puts the copper pot and ladle away and enters the hut. The man's gaze follows her. She is out again with a motley striped towel in hand, tosses it over his shoulders and is about to go away when he suddenly grabs her waist. She freezes. Hrisoula and I are watching. Through the thin shirt, the man's hands paw the woman's round ass and her calm, swelling breasts. Katerina leans into him. She is a stout woman as tall as her husband—they are an impressive sight, locked into each other like that. Both look back, then enter the hut still holding each other. "Why is he groping her so?" I whisper. Hrisoula fiercely bites her fist, looks at me with unseeing eyes, breaks a twig, and whips her bare feet.

I could not have known back then that the taciturn, fair-haired man will send my destiny in a direction away from the Karakachans. I did not know yet that people and circumstances appear in our life to steer us in the direction we are fated to go, which intersects with so many others that we can confuse it sometimes with somebody else's. If it was up to me, I would not leave the mountain for anything. I was used to living in it, freedom intoxicated me, Hrisoula kept calling me my girl, and I wanted nothing else. The fewer things some people have, the richer they feel, as long as, of course, they have the sky, the mountain and someone like Hrisoula.

The thing that changed all our lives, happened the following year. We were in the cabins in Eastern Thrace. It was summer again, only hotter and more sluggish than ever; here too the men slept in the open pasture, the women lived in the cabins, raised the children, rather kept an eye on them, made cheese in barrels with brine, washed the cans, cooked. Every night one of them welcomed her husband, the man whose turn it was to come down with the mules and white milk cans; she poured the water as he washed, spread a clean tablecloth on the dinner table for him, and after dinner they went into the cabin. They spent a long time there though it was still daylight, and the other women still chattered, wrapping up their domestic work and scolding the children. At dawn the man loaded the empty cans and led the mules to the pastures.

One evening I saw Hrisoula meet Yorgos again. No one was around when he grabbed her delicate wrist. This time Hrisoula did not step back, just smiled, whispered something into the man's ear and he let her go. She left him on her way down to the gully, shouting something in the direction of the women's voices and the clanking of pots.

The sun was setting and the wood was silent and peaceful. Hrisoula pulled me down to sit next to her on a warm stone. "What if the trees just go ahead and pull their roots out of the earth, how about this, eh, Pinyo? Look at their twigs, Pinyo, like wings. What if they just go and take off? Wow! This will be the highest justice ever. As for the humans who run on the surface of the earth not knowing what they are after, it's for them to get roots, don't you think, Pinyo? Then the Karakachans, all tired ramblers, will turn into a wood, a beautiful, calm, quiet wood. And I'll turn into a dogwood tree, thin and tough, that's my choice! Katerina's shadow is wide, she could be anything that protects. As for Yorgos, he'll be the tallest and proudest tree in this wood. And, you, Despino, you will turn into a low prickly bush, hiding blue crocuses, what do you say? We'll sit together, caress each other with our twigs and feel good because the trees are better than people! Of all nature, only the trees are not mean to each other! So let's do it, let's turn into trees!"

I protested and Hrisoula laughed. She took my hand and, now serious, looked straight into my eyes. "Listen, my sweet little girl. Let's just imagine we were trees, you—a prickly bush, I—a slender dogwood tree; now, without thinking twice, let's see what we'd do first if we pulled our roots out of the earth. We'd run away that very minute, that's what we'd do, and we'd roam the wide world. The memory of the human soul will urge us. We'll run down that path over there and vanish into thin air!"

As she was talking, her cheeks burning and eyes ablaze, she dashed towards the path, pulling me behind her. I started whining, but walked, though reluctantly, wading in a thick layer of dead leaves from several falls. We walked for a long time, right to the end of the sunset. It seemed that Hrisoula was really running away from something because she had no intention of stopping. We reached a steep cliff, climbed up and looked at the low land from above: in the middle of a round field we saw a village, its white cabins scattered like sheep. We climbed down to the field and there we met a woman.

The woman stood right in the middle of the dusty road pondering over something. Without a shadow of surprise, her eyes fell on us and she just sighed,

"It seems you've gotten lost."

"We were not lost, but not found either."

Suddenly the woman lifted her hand and laid it on Hrisoula's head—the palm pressed against the brow, the fingers slightly tapping the top of her head. The strange woman closed her eyelids tight and stood like that for a while. Silent and confused, Hrisoula didn't stir. The peasant woman stepped back, opened her eyes wide, and stared into Hrisoula's,

"Only chance led you to this path today, but you picked it out from all the rest crossing the mountain. It was your choice, so it's not a random one, is it! See, it brought you to me!"

The woman smiled and her face lit up as if it was washed in dew,

"I came to the field to talk with a flower. This morning,

still dozing, I heard it calling me. I felt it wanted to tell me something."

All of a sudden, she flung herself at our feet, one ear glued to the ground. She listened intently, then rose and beat the dust off her apron,

"I see it now, the direction is clear. That's the hardest thing to find, but once you do, the very path shows you the way … Truth is, lassies, they all think I'm mad. It's been about ten years now since I was blessed with this gift from God—to understand the language of all nature. Sometimes I talk with trees, with the tiny blades of grass, with the rain and wind, and I grasp all they say. It happens every now and then. The flower that's calling me now, that one over there, the little yellow flame, I heard its direction."

She walked straight through the dense nettle, skipped over the white stream, and bent over the flower in the meadow across. With a tense smile on her face, she stood there, stroked its fair head and came back to where we were. "Well, girls, I didn't quite understand this time, for it was not talking about me. It says we don't see our true dimension until we know love and suffering. We are here to know our real dimension. Not that I understand it all, but that's what it told me."

Hrisoula stares at the woman and the woman stares back. "Do you see now," the woman claps her hands, "you see why people meet? Because if they tread the same path, they can't help it! Farewell now and God bless you!"

The peasant woman turned around and rushed towards her village, whose white shadow was melting in the twilight. Hrisoula watched thoughtfully how the dust twisted its tail behind her like a ghostly dragon, and then looked at me, "How does it happen, my little girl, that people carry a gift so lightly without being in the least impressed by themselves and by what, through God's will, they have more than others. As if knowing the language of all nature is the most natural thing! Dear God! They called her mad, but I'm telling you Pinyo, it's like this: if you have a gift, you are not like those who don't have it. If you do, it's like you are not normal since the normal thing is to be like the others. It must be that people with God given gifts are the loneliest, oh God! Well, it's like this … Don't you think that God's gifts are meant to punish people? You would not feel free and at ease if you knew that sometimes God speaks through you."

My anxious feet were marking time.

Embarrassed by her own words, Hrisoula pressed the palm of her hand over her mouth and her azure glance shifted away from my face, her eyelashes fluttering.

Then, staring at her in turn, I spoke slowly and clearly,

"When I was a baby, there, in the red swinging cradle, I also understood the language of all nature. And when I was as lonely as the sky, I came to know my real dimension for a little while. It's true, Hrisoula, I'm not lying!"

Embarrassed by my words in turn, I pressed the palm of my hand over my mouth, just like Hrisoula.

The night was unbearably hot. Hrisoula tossed and turned on the straw mat; the leaves and straw in it rustled sharply. Drenched in sweat, I'd wake up occasionally, but immediately fall asleep again: the fatigue from the long walk proved stronger than the heat.

At dawn I felt someone enter the hut. I was about to scream, but I recognized Yorgos and, God knows why, pressed a palm over my mouth instead. Hrisoula sprang to her feet and faced the man. The moonlight had colored everything white and I saw the feverish glow in Hrisoula's eyes. The man spoke and her fingers touched his lips. Eagerly, he pulled at her shirt, wet with sweat, and I heard the noise of torn fabric as the shirt fell and bared her firm, pointed breasts. The scent of mint and wild roses spilled over and moaning wildly, Yorgos started picking the leaves stuck to Hrisoula's breasts with his tongue. She cried out, wrapped her arms around his neck, then quickly lifted her bare legs, glistening with sweat, and locked them around his waist.

Holding her hips, he pushed violently and they moaned in unison. Hrisoula threw back her head, her hair spilled, her supple body moved rhythmically. The man kept pushing and as if in a daze, she started whispering her hot, raspy sounds. It was unbearably hot and tense in the hut; I had no idea what those two were doing and I wanted to scream—much too early was I discovering about the closeness between a man and a woman. It rather looked like torture—so frantically were they biting their lips that they were probably bleeding. A scary thought flashed through my mind: Hrisoula could die, Yorgos is probably killing her. I would have screamed in horror but then I heard Hrisoula purr loudly and happily.

The last moans drowned in a fierce kiss, and I heard how their teeth clashed. Then the bodies collapsed on the bed and silence reigned. Gradually, their breathing became even and they fell asleep. As I thought over all that, I only vaguely began to guess what had happened and decided to ask Hrisoula on the following day. Then I slipped my hand under my cheek and fell asleep as well.

In the morning Hrisoula walked in a daze. Her lips were swollen and split, her eyes sparkled sharply. She tossed triumphant glances at Katerina, but managed to tame the bluish-green flames in her eyes by trying to focus on some work. Katerina ignored her, busy with tidying up, blowing the noses of the children with her fingers, stirring polenta, fanning herself with a kale leaf to blow the hot smoke off her eyes—calm and quiet, she did her routine domestic work. Gradually Hrisoula calmed down too and even looked somewhat gloomy, the light on her face fading. At dusk, she sauntered away and got lost. When she returned, she lay silently on her straw mat and stared into the distant, unreachable space. I sensed the surge of her anxiety and sadness around me and sat at her head. "Hrisoula," my voice came out serious, somewhat motherly. Hrisoula turned around, looked at me with desperate eyes and buried her head in my lap. So we sat, my fingertips caressing her hard curls as I just repeated … Hrisoula. Her name was like her. No one told me this, I found it out myself: only you can make your name singular and unique. Hrisoula's name was slightly husky, swaying like a bell of a wild flower when someone spoke it, purring like a cat, crisp when whispered. It was a smiling name. If the two sisters could exchange names, Hrisoula would sound serious, quiet and boring, and the name Katerina would immediately fit the little sister with her olive skin and high cheekbones dotted by the ponds of her eyes, her agility of a squirrel, the solid turnings of her hair, the thin, supple wrists, all that was hers. Whatever name Hrisoula was given, she would have made her name sound wonderful and unique.

Hrisoula calmed down enough to drink a ladle of milk and play a little with the kittens. I did not dare to question her about what happened in the hut at dawn. Days passed, my memories started to fade away, only occasionally the hut, bathed in moonlight, appeared in my mind's eye and I saw Hrisoula, clinging like a cat to the man: her naked, sweaty, glistening body swaying around Yorgos' hips, both secretly doing something pleasurable. I vowed never to mention what happened to anyone, but it was not ever repeated, not in the hut. Only sometimes in the nights when Yorgos came down, I sensed drowsily how Hrisoula slipped out at dawn and returned later smelling of cool, dew and happiness.

This lasted long. Both in Thrace and in the mountains above Sliven, Hrisoula and Yorgos continued to cling to each other; you could tell from the gleam in the girl's emerald eyes, which all but screamed with happiness on her olive face. From a skinny know-it-all she had become a young woman, even somehow soothed and settled. On the last trip to Eastern Thrace, I became aware that a new feeling was beginning to light up Hrisoula's face—it was an expression of constant wonder and delight as she grew more wistful and secretive.

And then something happened that destroyed the world around. And although rather small, this world was actually the whole wide world, as there was no other.

It was late afternoon. I was famished from roaming the hills and had missed lunch but it was early for dinner, so I slipped behind Katerina's hut, where the ailing sheep rattled its bell idly—the men had brought it down here because a snake had twisted around its udder, so the women had to put salve on the wound. I lay in the grass and started to suck the sweet milk, and as I did this, a thin stick swished at my legs. I tried to rise and dart away, but Hrisoula was faster; she pulled my ear and pushed my back to make me walk, her fast and angry talk made saliva sputter from her big mouth. On an impulse, I bit her. "Let me go, you, leet me goo," I tried to pull away raging like a trapped beast, but Hrisoula's fingers were iron hooks. She pushed me close to the fire where all the women had already gathered, knitting silently. Hrisoula pushed me again and I staggered towards the fire. The women continued to pull at the round balls of carded wool on the distaffs as if milking white clouds. Victoriously, her arms akimbo, Hrisoula announced,

"Look at her, have a good look and jeer you all! A big girl, could be married tomorrow, but still seeks to suck from the udder!"

The women did not react. Hrisoula's fury mounted and she whipped my mouth with the twig. Now, this was something I could not forgive. If we were alone, away from other people's eyes, I could have swallowed the insult, after all, I was guilty, but such shame was beyond what I could bear. I hated Hrisoula so much, I hated her guts and hissed,

"How about fighting and biting with Yorgos every night! Naked and all, there!"

Hrisoula was struck dumb. Her mouth open and arms akimbo, she just froze. The women looked up and slowly took the distaffs out of their bosoms. Katerina stood up, her face pale. She looked away, her eyes blind; not aware what she was doing, she pulled one of her children in front of her. Hrisoula came to her senses,

"It's not true!"

Katerina was silent. The women stirred at last. All eyes were focused on Marulla, the oldest. Marulla eyed Hrisoula with her small, weasel's eyes and puckered the bristling eyebrows on her low forehead, looking even more like a weasel.

"It's not true!" Hrisoula repeated

"We'll find that out," Marulla's deep voice answered.

Hrisoula rushed to flee, but they caught her and clustered around. Katerina, still silent, gathered the children, chased them away towards the gully, entered the hut, and never showed up again. The women closed in on Hrisoula, she tried slipping away into the bushes, but they barred her way, grabbed her skirt and bent over her. I could not see what they were doing to her; I just heard her scream. It seemed she was thrashing about, kicking and biting. Shaking all over, I ran around the ring of black skirts, trying to see what they were doing, and when I found a gap, what I eventually glimpsed made me lose my mind. Hrisoula was tossing in the grass, foam on her mouth, while Marulla stood above her trying to split her thighs open with her strong hands. Her undershirt was lifted, her naked body was writhing and the belly muscles convulsing. Marulla rolled up her sleeves and thrust her hand between the girl's thighs, then stood up.

"It's true."

The women were all hushed by now, you could hear a fly buzzing over the fire. Then I yelled, "It's not true, I was mad at her, I lied, it's not true!"

Nobody paid attention to me. As if on a cue, still bristling and silent, the women bent over the girl. Hrisoula's voice was no longer audible, only I howled, blue with terror.

"There is more."

This time Marulla's voice sounded so quiet and calm that my skin crawled. The voice sought the women's consent to something and their heavy silence gave it. Then I saw Marulla turning a bare spindle in her hands and splitting Hrisoula's thighs again. Hrisoula howled like an animal, and I bent over the fire and threw up in it, green, bitter poison.

The women brought Hrisoula in the hut and stretched her body on the straw bed. Marulla washed her hips with a wet apron, flipped down the undershirt, and tossed a wool blanket on top. She lifted Hrisoula's head, laid it on her folded elbow and poured a healing herb potion in her mouth.

The women filed out of the hut, each picked up her work. Only then did Katerina come. She stood at her sister's feet, hiding her face in her hands, "My baby sister, my little baby sister!" She knelt stiffly, raised her big hand, gently placed it on the girl's brow, dotted with sweat, and started whispering short words in quick succession. Curled up on the floor, I did not understand them, but I sensed that they were somehow ancient, special; the air around came alive and stirred. When Katerina's words ceased, I heard Hrisoula sigh. She was unconscious; the experience had shocked her and inflamed her brain.

Katerina stepped out, Hrisoula's wheezy breathing filled the hut. I started yelping like a wild cub, then the yelping turned into a quiet howl. Women came in now and again, but none sent me away; they didn't mind me and I howled undisturbed. The women changed the wet towels on Hrisoula's brow, brought honey, chicken soup, milk and forced them into the patient's mouth, opening her jaws with their fingers.

At dusk on the third day, Yorgos entered the hut and stood by Hrisoula's head; he reached several times before he could remove a lock stuck to her brow. Under the golden beard, his muscles twitched. He sat listening to Hrisoula's wheezing and then left.

I ran after him, "It's only my fault, Yorgos, kill me, stone me, crush me like a snake, it's my fault." He was deaf to my cries. He brushed the cheesecloth aside and entered the hut to Katerina. The rumble of his voice echoed and Katerina answered with a single word. A slap cracked. Yorgos came out and stood in front of the hut, staring at his feet. Then he headed for the woods, straight through the undergrowth, and never looked back.

In the evening, Katerina came again, her face swollen and purple under one eye. She stood over the patient's head, whispering her ancient, healing words, then sighed, briefly stroked Hrisoula's shrunken fingers and left.

The next morning Hrisoula stretched her whole body in a peculiar way, moaned blissfully and opened her eyes,

"Pinyo, is it dawn yet?"

Soon she got into her old routine around the house. She helped the women to strain and curdle the milk, got into playing with her kittens again, tried to comb my hair, tangled by the winds and hedges—she pulled the wooden handle of the ox horn comb, I whined, she scolded me, "Shut up and be patient now; as a woman by nature, you should be beautiful." Not even once did I hear any words about what I had caused with my lack of restraint, not a single reproach ever crossed Hrisoula's mouth: we had experienced a shock together and there was nothing to forgive. In some mystic way we were able to say everything with our pain-laden silence while she was lying half-dead in the hut. That there is something more powerful than words, I, Pinyo, realized then and there, and forever. I learned too early then that what cannot be spoken is louder than words. In moments of suffering, the unspoken has the power to give birth; that's right, we are born again, and if we can survive, we become new people. We both had become new people, Hrisoula—more pensive and preoccupied with herself, I—suddenly and irreparably grown. Katerina had changed, too. She had become even quieter. For all things, good or bad, she had always measured her words, but now she kept her mouth tightly shut. However, she had found the strength to forgive and her forgiveness saved from destruction both Hrisoula and her. We all survived, but each paid her price. It transpired that forgiveness brings relief to those who can forgive while the others are left to their own conscience.

Nobody knew what was on Yorgos' conscience. He did not come down to the camp for a long time; other men brought the mules. One early evening he came back, though. Covered in dust and sweat, his face flushed from the heat, he reeked of sheep. Katerina waited on him silently: she rubbed together a few sprigs of soapwort to lather the water, brought the towel from the hut, tossed it on the branch of a nearby tree, pulled down her skirt, and in her undershirt, straddled Yorgos, kneeling at the wash basin. She poured water with the wooden ladle and her fingers rubbed his ginger head, kneaded his bare back, she poured again, finally she threw the towel over him, rubbed his hair dry a little and stood up. She was drenched and steam was rising from her body. Yorgos pushed her towards the hut and she entered obediently. He lifted the cheesecloth strainer hanging above the entrance, lingered awhile and followed Katerina.

We had been watching them from afar, from behind the brambles, and I was afraid I'd see evil flash in Hrisoula's eyes, but she said nothing, only started to pick the dry burs clinging to her shirt. I thought she'd become indifferent until the night when I realized that it was just the opposite.

Marulla had sent me to gather brushwood for the fire. I walked deep into the woods, whistling, imitating the blackbird when I just stopped dead in my tracks: Yorgos and Hrisoula were facing each other at the other end of the path. I sneaked closer and heard the man gasp, "Hrisoula, I can't breathe without you, Hrisoula." Hrisoula moaned, wrapped her arms around his neck, they both collapsed and sunk in the tall grass. My heart beating madly, I returned to the fire and dropped the brushwood at Marulla's feet; she looked at me intently, but said nothing and I stepped inside. Panic seized me. Hrisoula, however, came back very calm. She jumped into the straw bed on her belly, waved a hand impatiently and I obediently slipped out.

Late that night Hrisoula shook my shoulders and when I screamed in fear, she put a finger on her lips, "Shush! Come on, we must go!" Startled, I was still lulled by sleep, but Hrisoula put a warning hand on my mouth and rather clumsily tried to dress me though I was long capable of doing the job myself. She took me by the hand and we walked out of the hut and down the path. We turned back for one last time just when Yorgos was leaving his family's hut and was about to tiptoe into ours.

"You'll have to learn to breathe without me, man!" Hrisoula said and we went on our way.

SOME EXPLANATORY NOTES FROM ELADA PINYO'S LAST FRIEND

I closed the last page of the first notebook with a cardboard cover and have to continue on my own, which makes me timid and insecure.

Of course all those four months turned out to be just this, only four months, and too short for Elada Pinyo to recall her life second by second as she wanted to. So, as she felt for the last time how grains of sand yielded under her feet, how the last glossy scales of her transparent skin shed and it grew thinner with no chance of recovery, how her body got even smaller, but the soul in it even more majestic, so the diminished body could hardly hold it, and as she felt all this as a festive, restless future, Elada Pinyo spoke her life as if in a trance, without order, without chronology as if the lack of order in her memories was of no special consequence while the swirling chaos of her experience created a new world for her, her own, and she was living it in real delight and real wonder; "Wow, is that me? Look at how I am, look at the people in my life, not a random pick, but unique, only mine! Wow, life is a mystery! Thank you, God, for giving me so much pain, which I turned into joy like you turned water into wine ..."

I listened through long days and nights, kept silent and remembered, remembered and kept silent, so from the debris, sighs, straws and trifles and from the scattered words of her passionate story I could try now to build up a decently clear story, with transparent detail, of this amazing woman and the characters of her people, distant but not at all random whom I, mysteriously, felt so close to my soul. If I succeed, it would mean that Elada Pinyo has given my faith unobtrusive guidance,

has shown me fiery words, has encouraged me, so we are one
here and beyond and the past can really happen tomorrow and
nobody can doubt it.

At One End of the Town of Burgas, on the Banks of a Swamp

At one end of the town of Burgas, on the banks of a swamp, stands a butchery. Tano, the butcher, is a small dark man with metal teeth, hairy arms with muscles grown too big with using the chopper and hands reaching down to his knees. The butchery is in the basement of the house under windows with red geraniums on the window sills. Very rarely, the oval face of the butcher's wife would peek from behind the pots. She'd look for a while at the film of green foam covering the swamp and further on, at the horizon beyond the sea, and then disappear for long.

Sometimes a skinny, fair-haired boy presses his nose against the windowpane. Then the woman appears beside him, watching him anxiously—her eyes, pitch black under the sickle-shaped eyebrows, glow feverishly. Her hair is like an untamed cloud of gold trying to sneak out of her white headscarf, hair that changes her in an unusual way, changes even her gait, straightens her up, so the woman doesn't just walk but somehow slides as if inches above the ground. The butcher's wife does not look Jewish but she is.

The boy's pensive eyes follow the flight of the seagulls; on the background of the sea, they usually look like white, flying blossoms but when the weather changes for the worse and the panicky fish hide in the depths of the roaring abyss, the seagulls, ravenous, rush like a pack of sky wolves towards the butcher's yard—they always find there piles of fresh, steaming offal, a prey they attack, furiously pick at and often lift in the air, the long, brown bowels hanging from their beaks. The boy watches, speechless. He goes back to his room, sits in the darkest corner, opens a book and sinks to its bottom; his face slowly relaxes and glows in a peculiar way as if sunlight spilled into an invisible well lights up his face and dances on his cheeks and forehead. Every now and then the yard echoes with the terrifying roar of an animal which the butcher first stuns with a hammer before using the knife. Then the boy starts reading out loud, and his voice keeps rising louder and more feverish, *like when you were a child, a little kid, you dreamed you were falling from a huge height or flying in the air, like the flying creatures do … you heard other voices, saw other faces … and stared into sunrises and sunsets quite different from those you see now or you saw sometime in the past which you could revive in your dreams;* the animal in the yard is choking under the knife, the butcher is scolding the apprentice about something, the seagulls hovering above screech shrilly, and the boy, his voice shaking even more, keeps enunciating the words clearly and distinctly, as if casting a spell somehow; *these visions are from other worlds, other realities, visions of things you've never seen in this very world; where have they come from then;* it's finally quiet in the yard and the boy is silent, too. He closes the book and pensively strokes the rough book cover for a long time.

Once, he had a lot of books, brought to him by his aunt Miriam from Spain. With the years, his father destroyed most of them, tore them up, crumpled the pages and used them to flare up the fire where the slaughtered pigs were singed. Only Scheherazade's tales remained intact and a little booklet entitled *The Space Wanderer*, which the boy had been reading in Spanish, his mother tongue.

Sometimes half-heartedly, he dares to ask for money for new books; he knows a bookstore in the town center; invariably, his father is immensely surprised, "Well, well, books, huh, books you say?" He doesn't add anything else and walks away, even more thoughtful, whistling skillfully because by nature he is a jolly guy, an expert whistler, and he can do two different things simultaneously, like being deep in thought and whistling cheerfully.

On the day the boy was fifteen, the mother put on her newest dress, with the lace collar, took off her headscarf and tamed the cloud of her hair with a wet comb. "Going downtown," she looks at the boy with radiant eyes; how peculiar her sliding stride is; impatient and victorious, today she slides much more than only several inches above the ground, more than any other day and look, she is already coming back, her eyes sending a kiss to the boy from afar as she lands with a slight sigh and thrusts a rustling packet into his hands. The boy feels the packet, his bright eyes thankful—his books are now four.

That evening while they were having dinner, the butcher, after swigging a jug of rich wine, put his hand on the boy's shoulder like a hammer, heavy and relentless.

"You're grown up now, so tomorrow, you'll start helping the prentice in the butchery because we can't cope with the work; it's a lot, God's been good to us, right? You'll work the tub."

The mother tried to object, the light on her face waned, the glittering cloud of her hair faded.

"He will go to school."

The father stood up, went to the open window and spat out,

"He will work. I started when I was ten, in the old

days."

The following day, the boy came back from school, went down to the butchery and stood silently by the door. His father was whistling and never looked at him. "You'll bring water here from the swamp and wash them until they are as clean as a new pin …" The boy was left alone in the back room, no windows, all cemented and dank, a heavy drop dripping monotonously from the ceiling. The deep tub is full of freshly cut lambs' heads.

He feels cold creeping up his flesh.

He stares at the blue, bitten tongues and the glazed, white eyes. He doesn't move; buried in the cement floor, his legs are turning into cement. The drop is still dripping from the ceiling, hitting the floor with a wet plop as if an invisible man was spitting from above. Suddenly the eyes in the tub become alive, scores of light blue baby eyes. Weak bleating fills up the room. The boy tries to dash out but his cement legs refuse to move; he strains with all his might, frees his feet from the floor and staggers out; the sun blinds him, hits his temples and the boy rubs them with his fingers—they are bursting with tension, both his temples, what would happen if the temples could see too … "God, I feel the pain has made them see, but I don't want to see so much."

The boy throws up in the bed with budding carnations.

In the evening the father paces back and forth in the room whistling the liveliest tune he knows, "Danube ruchenitsa," he announces, and then something occurs to him, "Stand up, let's go!"

The mother turns pale.

"No!"

The father drags the boy downstairs to the yard and

now into the butchery; the mother's steps rattle after them, don't, she enters breathless, stands in front of the boy, her thin body shaking. The man stares at her in complete shock, "You, obscure little Jew, don't you dare say a word! Just don't!" He talks to her in that way for the first time. The mother pulls her white headscarf down, crumples it in her hands and stares straight at the man, her eyes growing so big that they take up the whole face. The man is aghast, "You, miserable Jewish seed, shut up," but the woman has not uttered a word. He breathes alcohol in her face and she turns her head, "Ahaaa, the butcher's breath make the little white Jew squeamish, she prefers the smell of geranium, Greek gum and Arabic coffee; the stench of carrion and animal feces disgust her; the worthless little Jew forgets that with these here two shitty hands I bring the pure white bread on the table; if she doesn't know how to keep her mouth shut, I have to remind her."

With his back, the man pushes the boy out, bolts the door, the woman covers her face with both hands and keeps on shaking; the butcher comes back, "Now ... I'll remind you ... where you belong ... in this life ...," he grabs her under the hips, lifts her and topples her down on the butcher's table; the woman tries to push him away, her fragile hands thrashing in the dark like scared doves, oh, please; the man whistles fiercely, her dress hangs in rags, her white feet thrashing too and their radiance make the darkness around deeper and fatal. The man lies on top of her, the thrusts of his small, tough body shake the table, his heels dig the air, the smell of offal surges in from everywhere, pink and sweetish; turning her head aside, the woman tries to throw up, and the man erupts, moaning rapturously, how come he never thought of that table before; outside, the boy crouches in the bed of carnations, his fingers stuck in his ears.

At last, the butcher gets off the woman. His legs feel weak from the mighty thrill that still keeps his body twisting like a big earthworm; he staggers and laughs quietly. The woman remains lying on the tin table, her white legs spread apart. Her broken wings hang limp from her shoulders; the woman tries to fold them and spread them again, but fierce pain gnaws at her shoulders and she gives up. I'll make balm with honey, warm wax, a handful of ginger and horsetail extract; that'll cure them and then we'll see.

Outside, the man steps into the bed of carnations, lifts the boy by the collar, straightens him up; "Men, you male creature, have to study life like it were the alphabet: from A to Z; I'll make a man out of you."

The water drips heavily and monotonously. This is the heaviest water; the boy has heard that if a man stays under the drip too long, it will bore through his skull, squash his brain, kill him better than a bullet. It is dark in the cemented room, as dark as a bull's horn filled with tar and only the cut lambs' heads are showing white in the tub. The boy does not care anymore; he's petrified like a tree cut long ago and only his temples pulsate, trying to see, and suddenly the eye between the eyebrows opens, a third eye. The boy imagines feeling this place and senses a soft swelling. Right in the middle of his forehead is the third eye, no mistake about it, the all-seeing one, wide open and innocent, looking into the depth of a well filled with light. Somehow the boy knows that he's looking into himself and shuts both his eyes tight to see more clearly with the third. The pain in the temples has stopped and nothing distracts him. Every fiber in his body has sunk into deep rest. His back slides on the wet wall. The echo of the drop is far from here, but more powerful, different, bright and festive; listening to the song of the gigantic drop, the boy sinks into the well—the light there is soft violet like love that hurts sweetly.

And since his body has softened its bones and shut the valves of its blood, only light flows in his veins, his strong imagination tells him. Its strength is quickly wasted though, the light fades away, turns into gray mist and drains through the open eye of the well. His body stiffens again, fills with lead and when the boy tries to move it, he groans and opens his eyes. After the light, the darkness grows even thicker and stickier, and the boy notices how light makes darkness even more impenetrable.

The drop is still falling from the ceiling, the hollow, monotonous sound wakes up the lambs' heads out of their deep sleep and they start to phosphoresce in the dark; faint, tremulous bleating fills the room. The boy presses both palms to his ears and tries to go back into the well, but its light has faded and there is only darkness, hopeless and eternal.

He dashes towards the locked door, his fists pummeling at it. The silence on the other side of the door is indifferent and dangerous. Behind him the bleating turns into crying, frail and sorrowful. His fists are already bleeding, the silence behind the door is even more monstrous than the darkness here; the boy does not want to exist anymore, on either side of the door.

He rushes to the corner, sits under the drop, settles,

drip, drop, drip, drop, horrifically goes on to oblivion; his mouth lets out a sorrowful bleating which rises above the wavering sound of the lambs' choir, bounces off the four walls and the ceiling, the echo making it louder. He bites his tongue. I must be quiet. I must be strong. In the dark here, in the sticky pitch dark, I must be strong: real men, you male creature, should learn life from A to Z; he is right, I can't just sit, cross my arms and wait for the light to get out of the well and fill the world on its own so all is love again; I can't keep quiet anymore.

Dawn breaks. Roosters start crowing in the yards; their purple voices, husky and eager, rush into the darkness and peck his eyes with invisible hooked beaks. This is life, life exults around, he repeats the word, but does not grasp its meaning; the more he repeats it, the more meaningless it becomes. Since he deliberately kills the word, its meaning turns into the opposite of what it really means. The boy is ready to kill any other meaning until he is left with no words, because what cannot be spoken is stronger than words and now it can only be told through frail lambs' bleating.

When at dawn the mother crept up the creaking stairs and through the butchery opened the door of the cemented room, she found him, his tongue bitten, blue and hard as a stone, the back of his shirt soaked with blood.

The mother staggered and fainted on top of the boy.

"I did it because I didn't want you to grow up like this. I wanted you to be a strong man, scared of nothing in this life, this fucking life ... Books spoil man's soul, make him weak. It's your mother's fault because she buys those books for you, but little does she know that man is born a soldier because life is a war, a fight for survival, and you, with your silken soul, how can you survive?"

"I'm a simple man, son, I haven't read a single book in my life. But I'm not a villain. I even think I'm an honest man, and my work, nothing else, makes me so. You think I don't understand that I disgust you, my bloody hands disgust you, and your mother loathes me even more, like I've killed a man, not just brainless cattle that God has created for this. In Zelma's eyes I'm a cruel man, I scare her so much, I feel it, and I'm really cruel sometimes ... like then, forgive me, can you forgive me for that time? Zelma is a little Jew and her soul's white and I bent over backwards so she feels good ... I love Zelma and I love you, and my hands may be dirty, but the words I speak now, with my soul writhing, are pure; I never thought I'd share them. Believe me, both of you, I am not a bad man, believe me, so I am not a bad man ever again ... Fuck this life ... Don't you see how every Saturday I give meat to the poor for free, how I take care of their families ... I just think that work makes a man, not books, that's what I think."

"I'll give up drinking, too, I promise, because it straight goes and makes my head woozy and then, you see, I am worse than cattle ... and the cattle, you know, has no idea what it means to be a man, how hard it is ... so I'll give up the grappa, it's devil's work, and that night I was soaked, so everything happened the way it did. Trust me, son, I have a soul too, do you know how many songs I keep in it? I'll sing one to you if you want, the best: 'Stanka's face smells of lemon, lemon and yellow quince ; hey, Stanko-Stefanko, you spoiled city girl!' A beautiful song, right?

Like your mother."

"Forgive me, son."

"And your tongue, son, we'll cure; we'll find the best doctors to give you back the words, your live words; I'll go ask Zelma now to forgive me, but don't look at me, son, with those eyes, because we have to keep going …"

On the beach, not far from the town, a woman lives, her age is hard to guess. Her cabin's perched high up, hidden among the rocks, and down on the beach, her old boat waits for when she goes fishing deep into the sea if the weather is good. They call her the Fisherwoman because she is the only woman who does fishing for a living. The fishermen live in the bigger bay nearby, but the woman does not set foot there, nor do the fishermen seek her company because she can jinx their fish—word has it that she is a sorceress and exorcist.

One afternoon the Fisherwoman was quickly folding the nets she'd been darning. Clouds drifted in from the sea, leaned over the water like black sky rocks, and for no time at all, the whole area sank in darkness. The Fisherwoman piled the nets at the back of the cabin, went back to bolt the door and looked at the town from above—gloom hangs over the butchery; still lighted by the sun, the small suburbs beyond are calm and unsuspecting. The Fisherwoman stood still for a while, then turned around and surveyed the area again. Her eyebrows knit, her forehead puckered: down there a bright little figure fluttered, moving from stone to stone, creeping up the slope, sliding down and creeping up again.

Still not stirring, she waited for the man to climb up the slope. He was a skinny, pale boy. The boy stood before the woman, shivering in the cold. "It's not like you are the only person I miss here," the Fisherwoman blurted out. The rain started lashing down; the woman grabbed the boy's shoulder and pushed him into the cabin. She bolted the door, stirred up the fire, folded the nets. Only then did she turn towards the unexpected visitor,

"It's not as if I missed you, at all!"

The boy stood in the middle of the cabin; the woman lifted his chin with one finger, peered into his eyes.

"Oh, Lord!"

The tea in the cast-iron kettle was just boiling, the lid was jumping up and down; the woman poured yellow tea in a black pannikin and thrust it into the boy's hands. "Drink up!" He put the pannikin on the floor, sat next to it, and stared at the flames. Outside, the wind was raging, the rain lashing from all directions, the cabin shaking. The woman threw more wood into the fire, sat down herself and stared into the fiery tongues. A ginger tom-cat strolled by, stretched his back blissfully, and curled on the floor at the boy's feet. The Fisherwoman reluctantly broke out of her stupor, "If you think you've run away, that's entirely not true. You are where your thoughts are. The cat is here because his cat's thoughts are here, the reason he purrs so sweetly. I am here because I've learned to be here and nowhere else; believe me, it's true. People are in many places at the same time, so their souls can't find peace. Remember this and close those eyes of yours at last …"

"Because it hurts to look through them!"

The boy closed his eyelids obediently. The woman raised her hand and caressed him from a distance, without touching his face. She picked up the pannikin and started sipping. "Since you are already here, I won't ask you how you found the way; it's clear, the road itself has brought you here."

The boy's head drooped, but he sat up.

"Try to take a nap. Let your soul out of the hole where you've jammed it, listen to me!"

As he was sitting, he fell asleep. His body swayed from time to time. When he woke up, the rain had stopped and silence lay around. Only the surf could be heard, hitting the beach below.

The woman sprang to her feet, took the boy by the hand and lead him outside. The sun blinded them, late sun, washed by the rain. They walked on the muddy earth and reached the very edge of the cliff. Below, the sea was rolling its innards like a slippery, scaly monster. The woman relaxed and a smile lit up her weather-beaten face,

"See how great, how wonderful this sea of mine!"

The boy opened his eyes wide. It was his first time facing an abyss like this. He imagined walking along its edge, *the very edge of the abyss, walking the edge on one foot, slowly, above the abyss, and the world is a crumbling landslide, ugly, and I wheeze through my fish mouth,* some future song was rising in the boy, some future words were being born. There is nothing more tempting, nothing mightier and more startling than the call of the abyss. The boy heard that call and clung to the woman. She sighed,

"Many years ago, I wanted to jump down from this place, came here with that goal, crept on all fours, just like you a little while ago. See, even if my life depended on it, I would not remember why I came, not at all. I came here from a faraway village because I knew the sea would either kill me or save me. And I learned to manage my own time, to be here and nowhere else. What brought me to this beach is somewhere else and does not matter anymore. Trust me, it's true! It remained in my other time!"

The boy turned his eyes to her, the woman peeked into them again and again exclaimed impulsively,

"Oh, Lord!"

They stood above the abyss, holding hands.

"I wanted to fly down from the highest point, because down is the only way men can fly. Up they crawl, creep, strive, cling to thorns and grass, but down, they fly. Why do you think I perched this cabin up here, so each day I climb down the slope to the water and then climb up again? Not to forget that thing about the flying down being easier than the crawling up … Just remember, that kind of flight is an illusion. Well, boy, this is what man is, you see, until he comes to know time."

They walked back on the slippery road and sat on two stones in the sun in front of the cabin. The earth around was steaming.

"Since the road brought you to me, listen and remember what I'll tell you, I, a simple woman. People are wrong in their thinking about time. Those arrows are just spinning in that toy, the watch I mean, so it's not like time moves there—at least that's what they are telling me. But what if I just went ahead and crushed that watch under my foot, then what? Time is what moves inside man! But men, they go no, no, time is this and that and the other! Baloney! Who'll tell them that we are time's toys and we pass, time doesn't."

The boy listened to the Fisherwoman's rough voice

and watched how a pink worm was crawling up her muddy boot. He shuddered. "Don't be queasy, boy, just don't. Things in life are not always beautiful. But, listen to me about time, no, rather, look!"

The woman turned to the cat lying on a flat rock under the sun.

"Ps-s-t!"

The Fisherwoman hissed, the cat sprang up and darted towards the rocks: it all took less than a second. The woman nudged the boy,

"You saw this, my boy, that's it, this *pssst* is the present. Only this. It was and it's gone. While I was talking to you and before I spoke all my words, it'd already gone. Here comes the future, we tell it, *pssst,* and it goes and turns into past right away. Nothing is more frightened than the instant we call present, you know. So I learned to look only into the future, surging toward me; I learned to do this ever since I climbed up here to live on the edge of the abyss. I don't look back over my shoulder!"

The boy looked at her, his eyes begging. The Fisherwoman tossed her head back, "Oh, no, it doesn't happen right away and I don't know if it does at all, but it must be some gift, a rare gift, because otherwise all men would know how to look only forward, you see. It must be courage. It could be a strong character. Or it could be a dream, huh? Well, do you see now, you see, a dream! Ha! Listen, munchkin, I'll confide in you: I am sitting up here feeling lonely sometimes and telling tales, but, I think them up, then tell them loudly to myself, and if they're scary, I laugh; if they are funny, I cry and I suffer and I love them, the ones I create—I'm not lying, it's true. I'll tell you one of these stories sometime. So, this gets me thinking now, what if God creates us instant by instant, playing with us, so to speak, laughing and suffering, maybe loving us, that's what they say at least, but he could be dreaming us, what do you say, huh, what if man's life is God's dream? Wow! But don't be afraid, I told you I think up those things, all that fiddle-faddle ..."

The boy stood up and looked at the direction he'd come from.

"Ah, you're leaving. You climbed up the slope just to slide down on your bum. That's how it'll be. Young you are, too young, so that's how it should be. Let me tell you now about your future, the one I saw in your eyes. You'll be fine. Your words will come back to you. Without opening your mouth, you will speak more words than people with several snake's tongues in theirs; trust me, it's true. You have a long road before you, you'll see the world, meet people but neither the people nor your roads will be just random. You'll believe that man cannot control his fate, that fate controls man but you won't benefit a lot from this. A woman will look into your eyes, her eyes blue like yours, but it won't be soon, you're still young—when you are ready for her, she'll come. But pretty soon, you'll look into an eye, and it'll save you from the emptiness. So farewell and God bless! Go!"

The boy was about to climb down the slope.

"Hey, boy, don't forget that time is in you; because you are human, you are the time. We move time, not the other way around. Our hearts are the watches. However, some people cherish only the past time, others, the future. You have only the present stuck inside you, and it hasn't moved for so long, ever since what happened then, with your father. As for him, he did not do it because he was vicious; he is not that bad and he did it for your own good, because that's how he understands good. You just let the present turn into forgotten time, then you'll feel relieved, that's right. And stop thinking like you were a hundred years old because you'll end up with no time. Farewell and God bless!"

The boy left and never looked back.

He tried to run away several more times, but all his short escapes could not add up to a singular, life-saving one. Each time he'd come back with his head bent, stand behind the geranium pots, and stare long at the swamp and the flying white blossoms above it.

For some reason, he always tried to run upwards.

Once he managed to climb right to the top of the old poplar, the tallest tree in the town; only the fire station's tower was taller. He stood up there long trying to understand why he couldn't take his hands off the rough bark of the tree—he was neither frightened nor felt anything else, but his hands clung to it tightly. When he scrambled down, he walked like a paralyzed man making his first steps.

Once, he managed to escape from his mother's watchful glance during the service, ran up the three floors of the synagogue in one breath, and through the dormer window, stepped on the roof. He sat there, frozen in this position and did not budge while his mother scoured the nearby streets in search of him; from above, he was watching how her white headscarf was trailing on the ground behind her, how she stopped the passersby, wrung her hands and explained something tremulously.

Around him the pigeons fluttered noisily, cooed

throatily, darted in the sky and circled above the synagogue while down on the street the mother sat, her face buried in her knees; but then something made her raise her glance up to the roof, perhaps the pigeons, oh, my boy, man also needs wings to fly, strong wings is what he needs, heavenly wings for the mothers and their sons but mine are broken; I spread balm on them and I believe they would heal, and yours, son, are just showing; look how sharp your shoulder blades are, and now get down, my little guy; God bless your feet to cross the whole earth; hold on to the earth, son, because the sky just looks so near. The mother kept talking and talking to the boy, her pale lips tightly shut; she spoke in her mind, because she thought that he'd hear her better that way, yet the boy did not understand a word; even the words spoken in the mind were not familiar to him anymore, even his mother's words, the ones she spoke in her mind. His soul was empty and desolate like the Great Australian Desert, which he had read so much about; his soul was emptier than it: Aborigines lived and moved in it, reptiles crawled, haze flickered over the oases, but he was empty all inside. The boy got down to the street and walked with his head bent. A dove perched on his shoulder and flew away only when they reached the neighborhood around the swamp. The mother was walking behind at a distance, staggering from time to time, her white headscarf trailing on the ground behind her.

It's raining. A woman stands still and watches the rain with the eyes of a bird. The boys sneaks up to her and stares at the rain too. The house they stand by has a balcony and both are dry under it, a step from the water. It pours from the celestial pail, lashing the cobbled streets; bubbles form in the puddles and it's so joyful where bubbles pop and water ripples! The boy turns his face to the woman. She stands still and her bird-like eyes see through the rain. The boy grows pale. He can't take his eyes off the strange woman's face, no matter how desperately he tries. Minutes pass, hours, centuries. The boy shivers staring into the woman's frozen face. The woman rests her reddish hair bun against the wall and how extraordinary that during all these minutes, hours and centuries, her long lashes do not flutter, not even an instant. He suddenly wishes to kiss her straight in the open eyes, to ask for mercy. A raindrop rolls down the woman's cheek, "Do not look at me like that, it hurts when a boy your age looks that way."

The boy winces. He is just looking at the look in her eyes. He wants to explain how enormously frightening it is when a woman's eyes have that look. Some stray words come back to him, are born again, and bleed spurting out of life's womb. Unable to take his eyes off the strange woman's face, the boy turns even paler. *Have mercy. Your eyes look into other worlds; just make them look into my heart, and I'll kiss your warm eyes.* The woman does not look at him though it seems she's guessed his thoughts, "Other worlds exist, parallel to ours. Watch how the bubbles pop in the puddle of rain or look into the flames of the fire in the hearth and you'll see a crack leading there. I believe it's happened to you before, we all have this experience, but not all are aware of it. When you look into those worlds, your body freezes and time stops. Do it often, look at the winds, sunsets, candle flames, water at the bottom of a well; they are also a chance to escape, without a hidden danger to your body. Don't always get rid of your body, but just freeze it and get without fear into other worlds;

you are doing the opposite, going inside yourself but it is dangerous for a boy your age. The worlds I am talking about are also lit up and blissful and when later you hide into your shell again, you'll be stronger, and perhaps, wiser. It's not clear why since you've made no effort to achieve wisdom. But you will be all that, I swear."

The woman refuses to look into his heart, so the boy steps away from the wall and walks in the rain. "Don't resent me," she calls after him, "I am not the one to look into your heart. But you go, go straight through the rain; from all the people in the town, you now are the only one who does not hide from it. After all, the rain is just something wet if we watch it fearfully from aside, but if we stop being afraid, it's more than water, my boy; then, it becomes rain."

One night in his sleep, the boy turned into a real desert. The feeling was grandiose because he spread in a way that let him grasp the real essence of silence. He sensed no presence around, only streaks of sand waves from a past storm. Day and night did not exist, light and dark took turns causing no change, movement, memory. In a state of absolute ignorance, the boy felt blissful. He felt he was everywhere and everything happened at the same time, because even in this frozen state, things continued to happen. The Fisherwoman is right, the boy thought in his dream, retrieving the most important words, time is not what we think it is—here, a man can first die and then be born and this will be of no importance, but maybe, life and death happen at the same time and space rushes in later to separate them as they keep happening at the same time. In my dream, at least, but what if this dream became a kind of reality …

The boy dreamed and knew that his dream was more than a dream. It was the absolute freedom not to be. Or maybe, just the opposite—the absolute freedom to be nothing but himself. Just before turning into a desert, he dreamed his ever repeating nightmare; it was not even a dream but a naked thought which came alive every night and crept in the folds of his brain, infinite and fearful, a single one, but containing everything that could be known. His brain was bursting with the greatness of knowledge; unable to bear its might, the brain was writhing, powerless to contain this thought in the realm of the possible. And since it was all inside him, threatening to blast his wretched physical body, the boy wept in his dream, sorrowfully and inconsolably. At the time when his mind was as if about to explode, the endless desert rushed in, enormous and powerful. Then knowledge turned into blissful, absolute ignorance.

And the boy sighed gratefully. The desert also sighed from somewhere deep down and came alive; a sudden wind appeared, and stirred the sea of sand; sharp ginger grains of sand filled his eyes and reluctantly, the boy came out of his sleep. It was burning hot under his eyelids. He went down to the yard, scooped handfuls of water from the copper bowl and splashed his wide open eyes. He felt worse—his pupils were burning and sputtering yellow sparks; he felt how fine blood vessels crack in the sclera, so he sat on the ground and stared at the night sky with his bloodshot eyes. Stars were shining, the moon was hiding its oval face under a green veil and peeking out pensively every now and then. The boy gazed up for a long time. He had come back from somewhere up there. He tried to interpret the lesson he was given: once achieved, if at

all, knowledge turns into primordial blissful ignorance—
perhaps somebody was trying to put into his head the idea
that he should not be scared of either, and that sometimes
not knowing is not ignorance but simply a safe haven for
a curious, impatient mind. His was achingly impatient
to learn the secret of all secrets, but, just like the moon
above, the secret unveiled its face only for an instant; it
made the boy squint at its dazzling might, collapse in the
foothills of its sky and ask for mercy, and in an instant, it
veiled its face again.

He could not do anything but wait for the next instant
to frantically utter his short human prayer—*tell me who
I am*—he knew too little for now; he suspected that all
knowledge exists in man, but life outside man contains
the diverse circumstances that can urge the soul to look
in the right direction. Or in the opposite one. Somebody
was trying, it seemed, to make him believe that at a given
moment, aghast at the grandiose incomprehensible, man
voluntarily has to let go and rely on arbitrary fate and that
was the right thing to do for the moment; he knew it was
too early to ask, too early for his age.

He stood up and looked a little longer at the brightening
sky. Then he walked out of the yard and started to cross
the street. The little windows of the pastry shop across
were still lit up. The boy went and pressed his nose against
the window: Manyo, the Greek, is leaning over the table
kneading dough, her body sways rhythmically, her bare
arms bend, turn and twist the rising sea of dough; a cloud
of sighs, scents and warmth hovers around her ginger
head, and the boy feels that through the window. Next to
the oven, lying on the wooden bench, Ferso, the baker's
daughter is taking a nap, her red hair streaming towards

the floor, her chin with the deep dimple vibrating, and as he is looking at her, the boy smiles spontaneously. He scratches the glass with a fingernail, Manyo lifts her head and a smile lights up her face, too, "Come on in!"

The boy entered, sat on the chair beside the sleeping Ferso, leaned his back onto the warm wall and shivered, sensing only now how stiff he was from the morning cold. Manyo continued to fight with the pile of dough, flashing a glance at the guest from time to time, warming him with her smile; the bliss of sleep was a distant memory now; the pale morning light, restless and eager, poured through the steamy windows, and the boy shivered again: could I be dreaming this time—Manyo, the warmth of the fire, and Ferso, could reality be the real dream sometimes? He was aware that it was dangerous for a boy his age to ask questions beyond his age, even if while dreaming; he wanted to be like Manyo and Ferso, like all ordinary people in the world.

Strangely enough, at the routine checkup, doctor Bedros first looked into his eyes *if only he wants it, perhaps, he can speak one day;* the mother was crumpling a silk kerchief in her small hand and did not want to look into her son's eyes. When they walked out of the doctor's office, the boy took her by the hand and led her along the uneven cobbled street. They reached the synagogue, where the pigeons fluttered and their cooing made everything around white and quiet. They passed by it and reached the little bookstore; the mother tried to lead the wobbly synchrony of their steps towards it, towards the words, her hope fragile but the boy turned his head away. They reached the quay: small ships were blaring, dazzling seagulls flying, the air smelled of salty iodine and seashells;

they walked a while on the carpet of shells, crunch, crunch, the big guy and the little woman, with the same bottomless eyes; when they returned to the ships, the boy pointed at a ship with his eyes and the mother read out loud *Regina Spain.* She knew and her glance shrank and withdrew inside as if a spring sank into the sands; Regina Spain, why so far away, she groaned inside, but came to her senses, he is far away even now.

"Very well, I'll write a letter to Miriam but it'll take time."

They went back to town and entered the orthodox church. It was dim inside; the flickering flames of the candles moved the air and the whole church swayed in the surge of light. They lit their candles, stared into the heart of the flames and did not move their eyes off them until the wax got soft and drooped. The boy kept on looking at the empty space, as if he had left himself—God, does he have any words left, at least for prayer! The boy prayed without words, staring at the memory of the candle's flame; life had hushed in him again, shrunk to the size of a white dot, no bigger than the memory of the burned out candle.

"Why not in the synagogue, why did we walk into the orthodox church … God, he is praying for him, not for himself." The boy was still staring into the eye of the candle, which the mother was quick to light again with her shaking hands; the eye started weeping with hot wax tears and at last the boy found some hard, silent words, "Oh, please, cry for him, cry for me and my mother, I beg you, cry with the hottest tears in the world, please, if you think that God should cry for men, cry, God!" The hot wax drops fell onto his hand, cooled in thin crusts, left no traces.

They walked out of the church and started making their way through a crowd of people, dusty and gloomy; "Refugees from Edirne," the mother explained, "chased away from their houses and churches, they left their life there and are without a life of their own now." The boy stopped to watch how the refugees were filing into the church: the men took off their caps at the gate and pressed them to their chests, the women all stared at the ground like women do at funerals though now nobody was being buried. "Maybe, they have come to God to help them to accept their fate," the mother said, and the boy thought he was a refugee, too.

All of a sudden, among all the silent people on the square, a girl fluttered like a blue butterfly. Blue is her skirt, bluer her eyes, her face with high cheek bones is tinted by wild winds, her hair is bluish black, but even bluer in the sun, "Wow, what a church!" the girl wonders and bumps into the boy, "Sorry, my fault, pardone moa, it nice, that church, no good Bulgarian me speak, zhou perl un peu, un mal, I speak just a little," the girl's bright eyes sparkle, she spins around and claps her hands, "Nice town Burgas, very." She flies away out of the range of their eyes with her blue skirt, with the blue in her eyes and the joy she's put in her hair like a white hollyhock.

The day is dying; the boy and the mother look around, their eyes seeking the girl—"But I am a Bulgarian, Bulgarian," she smiles from afar and sinks in the crowd, a whirlwind of bluish dust twisting up from under her feet.

The evenings are lucid; snow sparkles crack in the sharp air. The hungry seagulls circle above the butchery and caw like ravens, their curved beaks rummaging the fermenting piles of animal carrion. The boy puts earplugs in his ears and presses his palms against them so he won't hear how after dinner his father, having drunk a bottle of grappa, scrambles down the wooden staircase to the butchery; how after a long silence his mother's steps shuffle down, heavy as stones, as if the Sphinx from the book about the pyramids is making his first steps in the house. The boy does not hear how later the butcher's table starts shaking and creaking, nor does he see his mother lying crucified on the cold tin sheet covering the table, her wings hanging from the sides, snow white and crippled; "Hug me with those arms of yours, Zelma, why do you hang them like they were broken," the man sulks, his feet rake the air, the pink, sweetish smell of butchery fills the woman's nostrils; oh, God, she starts throwing up like the first time and so as not to choke turns to the side and empties herself, her mouth wide open until the last convulsion of her terrified insides; the man also comes, his twisting body pours the warm white fluid onto the woman's belly, "Look how strong it is, like ox's milk, look, look, looook," he howls, then steps off her, wobbles, soft in the dark, walks out to the yard and pees in the carnation bed; the powerful flow squirts out and the man quietly laughs, "I am like an ox and my pee is like a bull's, and my strength too; I might be small but I am tough; Zelmaaaa, hear my pee, someday I'll pee it in you, I'll set you on fire with it like it were gas; by gad, Zelma, I'll do it for real if you still lie under me like a cripple …"

He is climbing the stairs, tamed.

The woman manages somehow to fold her laden wings, wipes the vomit off her face with the skirts of her messy dress, scrambles to the floor and walks out, her posture straight, her head up. She stumbles stiffly now and then, the seagulls caw above her and their feverish choir sounds all the way to the swamp, where the woman wades up to the waist in the cold water; when she walks home, her posture is still straight; although she shivers and a small dark rain trickles down from her, she is in no hurry to go upstairs; she kneels at the hollow of the dead walnut tree, takes out a halva box filled with balm, special balm for crippled wings; she pulls the rags off her shoulders and starts rubbing the balm on them; her left hand rubs the right shoulder blade, her right hand—the left; tenderly, carefully, she touches the roots of the wings and they hurt like rotten; then she puts the halva box back into the tree hollow and pulls all the rags back on; tomorrow he will apologize and buy her a new dress, even more expensive, but now she will just wrap her wings, her fluttering snow white wings, around her and climb the stairs with heavy steps like a clumsy stone sphinx.

One day, the boy walked out without telling anybody. It was already winter, icy film covered the puddles and they cracked under the feet. He walked for a long time, following his feet.

At the fire station, joking and laughing loudly, the firemen were hanging around the pumps, loaded on two-wheeled carts. The boy looked up at the tower, the highest place in the town, and stared hypnotically for a long time.

A horse snorted; they had let the animals run around free for a while. The boy went in. A mustachioed man winked at him, a shaggy dog pranced around and put its paws on the boy's chest. Light snow was falling, the first that year. The men went back into the building; only the mustachioed fireman and the horses remained outside. One of the animals pricked its ears, widened nostrils, inhaled an enormous gulp of air, then exhaled and clouds of warm vapor wrapped around its head. The horse was black and shiny, with a little white flame on its head. The boy drew closer and felt its warmth. The horse stood still and the boy gazed into his big moist eye. A snowflake flew into the eye and that moment shook the boy. It was a cosmic moment, a whole universe in a moment—he felt its boundlessness, but did not lose himself in it. He sensed a sudden bliss filling him, without any obvious reason. The desert in his soul bloomed, distant waters rippled, the sky dazzled him, and all this—because he saw through the eye of the horse.

He came out of his trance and leaned his forehead against the horse's rump; the horse whinnied and lowered a frosted eyelid. The snow was falling faster, the mustachioed man led the horses to the stables. The boy lifted his head to the fire station's tower and saw a green beacon of light was coming out of it. He thrust his hands into his pockets, huddled his snow-laden shoulders and headed home, his steps light as if he'd grown wings.

The pigeons on the roof of the synagogue coo white silence. Every now and then they shake their wings, downy fluff flies up, and the tiles on the roof look even frostier than the earth because the pigeons at the synagogue are all white, every single one of them.

The dove Zelma is on the roof with the other doves and her bottomless eyes look at the sky. She knows that it's not so near as it looks but far away and only doves with strong wings can reach it, while she, Zelma, is not quite sure in her wings, their roots painful, hurting as if rotten, but it's time, yes, it has come because the boy with the bottomless eyes needs to forget the sight of the poor, violated body; it's his time to understand that the body does not matter and neither does the following scene: her torn dress all in rags, her legs shining in the darkness and brown urine pouring over her thighs; "I did it, Zelma, because you refused to hug me with those wooden arms of yours, you see now?" the guilty earthworm Tano is squirming above her, erupting poisonous grappa; the woman is throwing up her hopeless insides, the table's shaking, the boy with the bottomless eyes is watching from the doorstep, then suddenly clings to his father's back and his blind fists pummel his back, his head, the air, and because the scene had left no strength in him, it's easy for the man to throw him off with just a flip of his strong shoulders, "You … damn puppy …," the man gets off the woman, takes him by the collar, throws him out in the yard and bends over him, his dick still leaking, the drops falling into the bed of carnations, "I said I'd stop, I said so, but you little puppy, you would never be a man, not until you learn what life is from A to Z."

Getting off the table, the woman feels cruel pain gnawing at her shoulders; then the pain suddenly subsides and she feels no pain for once—her wings get lighter, all bright fluff and soft surge; Zelma wraps them around her body as she gets off the table: she needs her wings to protect … She walks to the boy and embraces him with her tender, white wings, "Shuush, quiet, quiet, my boy," though he does not make a sound, "Your wings are coming out, too, don't you feel them? Look how sharp your shoulder blades are; who knows, maybe the sky is not as far as I think, shuuush, nothing happened ... If I don't want it and don't partake in it, it doesn't actually happen—each time I fly on my crippled wings up to the ceiling and just look blankly down and that scene is nothing, believe me ... It's what snails and cats do, dogs and lions, too; we try to imitate them, the animals that we are, all of us, and that's all; maybe, God has deprived us of wings for the original sin ... It must be that ... He's taken our wings but I'm sure we belong to the flying species; otherwise, why would men think up airplanes, shush ... quiet, my boy, don't cry so, such dry crying hurts and it's not worth it to hurt for all this; do not cry for the ugly things because other, important things happen in life, then you can cry with real, grateful tears for their greatness, for the miracle of their existence ... Don't worry about me because I am strong, I have wings, my boy, so you shouldn't cry but rejoice, for my obedience is just superficial; it is because I still pity your father, but also I expect a lot from him ... Now let's go upstairs to your room and I'll read to you about the star wanderer; I need to go to the swamp first and I'll be back and everything will be as before, I promise you, because we both have the same eyes, my boy ..."

Now Zelma the dove is on the roof of the synagogue with the rest of the doves, waiting for the service to end, the people to leave and when the boy, who is probably wondering where she's disappeared, steps out, she'll spread her wings and at last the miracle will happen, because it is very important that the boy know great things can happen in life.

It was his last day in Burgas. The following morning he was leaving for Spain on a big ship; his aunt Mariam was going to meet him midway, in an Italian port town.

In the spring morning, the town was reluctantly waking up: lazy cabriolets clattered; milkmen and newsboys half-heartedly hollered, the sun, jagged from the cold, was trying to sail above the sea. The boy walked aimlessly, saying goodbye to the town … He reached a two-storied house in the quiet center and stopped at the gate with the tarnished brass ring knocker.

He stood at the strange gate for a long time. The walls pulsated with the palpable energy of home and suddenly the boy wished to have lived here and nowhere else. He felt numb, he couldn't lift his feet to make a single step.

When he finally found some strength to move and made the first step, he noticed that the east side of the house extends into a porch, overshadowed by a black vine; on the porch, a man in a wicker chair was trying to set up a tripod of a kind. The boy went back to the door and knocked, his heart pounding in his chest. "Come in!" the man yelled, not turning his head. The boy stepped up to the porch, sat in the other wicker chair, placed his palms on his knees. Even now, the man did not look at him but started feeling around him. He can't see, the boy guessed right, he is sightless. "Pour some," the blind man nodded at the jug with ayran on a low table. The boy poured some in the glass, took a sip and his teeth tingled from the sharp taste. The man put on the tripod a piece of taut canvas on a wooden frame; "You've never seen anybody like me, right? I bet you haven't met a blind artist so far!"

The boy took another sip from the ayran, a piece of ice crunching between his teeth. "I have an icemaker in the basement, I supply the whole town. Why so silent for such a long time, can't you speak?" The boy couldn't answer and the man wondered, "Well, well … out of both of us, my dear guest, they could make a complete person; we just need to find out how." Only now the boy could see his face: the high forehead plowed by deep lines, the high cheekbones and the grey beard, the narrow eyes stretching to the temples, with pupils burned down to white. The man stood up, walked to the boy, reached out and his fingers felt his face. "I saw you. You should know that God does not bring people together just like that. You've come, so you need me … or, maybe, I need you—probably we both need each other …" Touching the brushes with his fingertips, he was arranging them in a clay jar. "I draw the world, in order not to forget the world. I got retinal detachment after a bad flu, so my sight is weak; I see only shadows and large spots of color. It's enough as long as I can draw … I lost my sight, little guest, and I became a different man—I'm telling you the truth, you can trust every word. When your body changes, what's inside the body has to change as well. There's no other way. Compensatory energies are put in action, that's what happens. I started to see the inner; it's lighter and brighter than the outer, trust me." *The well,* the boy thought. "Before, I was teaching art in the Armenian school; I painted in my free time, and I thought that I was a decent artist but, in fact, I had no talent though I did not know that, just like the fool does not know that he is a fool and the talentless that he has no talent. Come, I'll show you."

They entered the artist's shop. Along the walls, many canvasses were arranged, with their backs up. The blind man went to one of the walls and started turning the pictures over. "These are from before." The boy saw green mountains, blue seas, brown horses, white swans.

"Do you see, my little guest, what a tautology. Complete lack of talent. I had my sight, but I did not know that each thing is more than it looks."

The man started turning over the pictures leaning on the wall across. Rough spots of color. The boy strained and with effort was able to distinguish gnarled trees upside down, green gawky horses with square necks, sharp red grass, violet seas … Weightless objects in space: boats in the sea almost perpendicular to the waves, ready any minute to dart into the air; a heavy, black cow lying in a puddle, drawn in a single stroke, and white calves, clinging to the huge udder, bigger than the calves; a man standing on the edge of a sharp tooth of a cliff, ready to fly over the abyss, drawn with a single flip of the brush, a single clumsy stroke. The boy recalled the Fisherwoman's words that only people could fly down; it was obvious that something was holding the man in the picture on the edge of the abyss; it was clear that he would not succumb to his dark impulse but stay there, on the edge, all his life. The boy shuddered. The artist turned the pictures towards the wall. Then he repeated again: everything is much more than it looks …

After each had another cup of ayran, the boy left. He was walking with his shoulders bent thinking that the people he had recently met had something in common, as if they were relatives by blood but knew nothing about each other. The way they spoke was similar, as if they were one person, but with many faces. Maybe, that's how it is in life, a few similar humans create a whole, no matter where they live or if they know each other … They may even take no interest in each other but still complete each other, exchange invisible energy and unite. Maybe, as the

Fisherwoman had told him, the people he met were truly his people, and, maybe, they guided his soul to look in the right direction as they resembled each other in one thing: they had the ability to enter the well of light.

However, the boy was not sure if he still needed that since he had gotten tired of his own life and intended to leave it for the time being.

The ship blares, its chimneys belch clouds of smoke, the air smells of burning coal, its metal body vibrates with the impatience of the travel bug. The boy is on board with the rest of the passengers and is looking at the shore. The people who have come to see others off have stopped bustling and also silently watch the passengers. In fact, the journey has already started, although the ship is still at anchor. The boy's eyes search for his mother but see his father first: shrunk under his guilt, Zelma's forgiveness, and the alcohol, which he still craves but wouldn't touch for anything on earth since then, Tano, careful and compassionate, escorts the boy's mother, but she is silent—her small body, hanging from the crutches, is swaying as if ready to jump although it can't happen; the boy strains to see her eyes: her glance rushes in like a high tide. Suddenly, things begin to happen simultaneously.

Spring is everywhere around, the water in the harbor sparkles in the sun, all the passengers have their hats on, and Burgas' sky is unbearably bright ... *only over the synagogue, big snowflakes fell and piled on the roof and the doves fluttered their wings fearfully, spilling down the snow from the eaves and then Zelma Dove flew off the edge of the roof; the air stirred with a hiss and blew the flared skirts of ... her coat; the scarf on the shoulders ..., whiter than the snow, blew up too and time stopped; the people stood still and did not utter a sound; only the doves cooed restlessly and everything turned even whiter under that sound, and Zelma was flying smoothly and the boy could see from below her bottomless eyes, the powerful strokes of her wings; he could hear the ends of her white scarf swish, and he could swear even now that his mother made an elegant lap above the people's heads, before cutting heavily into a deep snowdrift.*

Zelma and Tano wave once more, turn around, and leave. They walk away slowly and the boy looks after them until he can hardly distinguish his mother's sliding stride, only the strokes of her crutches slashing the air. Tano follows her, vigilantly watching over all her movements, ready to offer his help with deliberate compassion. The two of them hide behind the corner of the little square across and the boy turns away to look at the water—olive green and sparkly in the sun, it has the strong, bitter smell of childhood. The carpets of sea shells remain on the beach, the black slippery rocks, the horses at the fire station and the jolly firemen, the Fisherwoman and the woman in the rain; Manyo, the pastry cook, and Ferso, with the fiery hair and the dimple in her chin, the blind artist and the blue girl in the crowd of refugees, her joy pinned to her kerchief like a white hollyhock, and the golden Burgas sun shining above all except above the synagogue, where the snow was still falling and piling up, and the boy was beginning to guess that up until the end of his life, this snow would happen together with everything else in the world.

They were in front of a big town, sunk in a shallow valley. From the hill where they stood, it was hard to see the roofs in the morning twilight; only one neighborhood was climbing up a steep slope, the houses perched one above the other. The dawn was breaking, but the street lamps were still flickering. The town was asleep.

"Here you go, Pinyo, your town." With a sweeping gesture, Hrisoula ceremoniously gifted it to her. Your town on four hills: three rivers flow into each other nearby, all named after women, Arda, Tundzha and Maritsa—in this town lives the honorable Vassilaki, the furrier, he'll give us shelter …"

They had been walking for several days without direction; Hrisoula was following the sunrise and managed to lead Pinyo to the valley. They slept during the day, moved at night and were not scared of anything, except people,

"People are all sorts, Pinyo, God's created a colorful world under one sky—good and bad, honest and mean, all sorts and all want to live under one name, humans, that is."

They had arrived at last and Hrisoula boldly headed for the Christian neighborhood. They lingered at the high gate, then the woman mustered her Karakachan courage and knocked on the door with the brass ring.

"Here they wake up early and won't be cross," she calmed herself and beamed at the small mustachioed man, who sullenly opened the door, yawning so widely you could see his tonsils.

"Who are you?"

"Well, we're Pinyo and Hrisoula."

"So what if you are?"

Hrisoula was stuttering: she used to come here as a child with her father, they brought furs and cheese, but he died ten years ago, then her mother followed and now she had to look for a job,

"Please, master Vassilaki, you are like a father and mother to us!"

"Who's this little thing?"

It's Despina, or Pinyo, I told you.

"And this?"

Under the blue, loose-textured headscarf, the basket in her hands moves, comes alive, plays. Hrisoula smiles and the smile lights up her tired olive face:

"My cats!"

"Crazy lass!" To bother him here with a child and a whole litter of cats, and believe on top that he'd take her in. Didn't he have a head on his shoulders, he had no use for a maid, even the cats would be hard to feed, did such a thought ever cross their minds, "I am not a Karakachan in the mountains, I don't have milk! Why did you leave your woods?"

"Don't ask me, master Vassilaki! It's none of your business!"

Vassilaki was about to go back inside. "Please, man," Hrisoula started begging, her bright eyes focused on him. "Take me so we won't starve and we'll work just for the bread! This child is on my hands, and I don't want her to die!"

If she'd throw away the cats, he could think of taking them in for the winter, then they had to go their own way, but, first the cats, the cats he did not want …

Hrisoula fumed,

"I'll throw them, I'll drown them in Maritsa! You just watch! I'll skin them alive! You just say you take us, I'll rip their heads off!"

The furrier waited until her outburst subsided,

"You do this job first, and then we'll talk."

And he slammed the gate in their faces.

Hrisoula grabbed the little girl's hand and dragged her along. Far out of town, the three rivers crossed but it was as if they were many more—wherever you were headed, you stopped at water. They reached a beach, sat down, caught their breath. Hrisoula uncovered the basket, the kittens jumped in her lap and started licking her hands one after another. Together, the girls ripped the headscarf into strips and tried to use them to tie stones to the kitten's little throats. They meowed wildly and resisted but somehow, Hrisoula managed to do the job. She looked around to see what she'd done, then clapped her hands and goggled her eyes, "Well, look now, Pinyo, how about you go ahead and throw them, huh!"

"Ha, do I look like a killer? You came up with this, you throw them!"

Hrisoula raised a fuss to the sky; she was not a killer, she was just wondering how to cope with the situation; she'd have to choose between Pinyo and the cats, there was no other way out. And because the girl was giving her the evil eye, she clapped her hands and goggled her eyes even more,

"I'll throw you in the river, shorty!"

Then she laughed, "The best thing would be to throw master Vassilaki in the Maritsa, to tie a stone on his neck and—plop! Drown the cats, he says, I don't want them! Skin them alive! Rip their heads off! Am I crazy, to kill my kittens! We'll do without master Vassilaki, right, my girl?"

They scuffled and landed on the cool sand, feet up. Their laughter had not rung like that for quite a while. The cats were running to and fro with the stones on their necks and screaming in panic. It was fun, and to crown it all, the sun rose and the day shone, pink and clear.

The fun was in full swing when a big male voice startled them,

"Hey you, little butchers!"

They jumped up, strengthened their shirts and looked uneasily at the dark, curly-haired man who was standing on the shore above them: his huge body hides the sky, a cart drawn by a red colt has stopped behind him and a girl with an enormous, swollen head sits in the cart. Hrisoula came to herself and started a lively conversation with the man; Pinyo and the girl in the cart watched each other intently, the colt snorted and sneezed and Pinyo felt that something nice would happen, sensed it with her whole body, bristling in the nippy air.

The man listened patiently to Hrisoula and ordered, "Untie the stones and take the cats." As everybody rushed to catch the younglings, the little girl in the cart continued to observe the fuss silently, her head swaying on her long thin neck like a huge dandelion. The man threw two sacks at them, "Get down to work! One of you holds the sack, the other fills it with sand, and I'll sift it through the screen."

After loading the sacks into the cart, the girls sat on top of them, and the man lead the colt. They stopped at a big house in the Christian neighborhood, in the very center. The man opened the gate and they entered into a cobbled yard with a garden and a well. The house was on two floors with lots of windows; at the far end of the yard stood a low, long building where they unloaded the sacks. It was spacious inside, with a brick furnace hunched in the middle. The door to another room was open and they could glimpse the high tables and shelves where sparkling objects were arranged. "I am a glazier," the man caught their glances, "haven't you seen glass? I'm Ovanes, and I want to hire you. You will help me raise my daughter and around the oven," he cut a glance at Hrisoula. "The girl will be Syruie's friend, they'll play together."

The two girls timidly entered the house. They were amazed at the bright glitter coming from some flat, round glass objects on the walls. "They are mirrors," Ovanes noticed their astonishment, "look in them, if you want. You will see yourselves as you really are." They approached reluctantly, stood in front of the nearest mirror and looked. They were both shaggy, black-haired and bright-eyed, suntanned and dusty. Stunned, they looked at themselves. "Listen, Pinyo, little devil, we sure look alike! Is it by nature or by reflection? When two people constantly look into each other, who knows, they may start reflecting each other? Say, like mirrors …"

"I wonder if you'd reflect your own mother that much!"

Hrisoula suddenly raised her skirt high above the knees and flirtatiously spun around in front of the mirror. She was all aflutter, "Ha! look at me! It's true, I am like a dogwood tree, so thin and so tough!" Pinyo recalled her supple, naked body twisted around the man's lap.

While Hrisoula was admiring herself, the girl was looking around the house. She'd never seen such wonders: thick carpets on the floor, heavy tables with lace tablecloths, carved armchairs and couches. And a lot of glass objects. A wide wooden stairs lead to the upper level. Syruie climbed up the steps, her head swaying on the thin stem of her neck. "She is sick, has a water head," Ovanes explained gloomily. "Her mother died after giving birth to her and I raise her alone with the help of nurses; the last one left a week ago. I want to warn you that she is a difficult child, quiet and of gloomy disposition. Her soul's fragile, though, as if made of glass, so be careful."

And Ovanes started to teach Hrisoula how to take care of the girl.

Pinyo stood next to a tall narrow table, a jug full of water sparkling on it. Water head … She imagined the girl Syruie carefully climbing the stairs, her tender neck carrying not her curly, swollen head, but this transparent jug instead, full of water. As if hypnotized, Pinyo watches how the liquid in the jug sways as if a beam of sunlight has sunk in and rocks it, and she thinks: if the glass breaks, Syruie will live only a short time. Why is that thought crossing her mind, she has no idea. Without knowing what she's doing, she pushes the jug off the table; it falls and breaks into pieces with a ring and the water runs on the carpet …

Hrisoula clapped her hands, took the new green headscarf off her neck, and started to soak up the water from the puddle with it, while also scolding Pinyo in a low, angry voice. Ovanes stopped her from slapping the girl, "It's ok; don't worry, plenty of jugs here … but still, beware, you're not elephants, are you! And you, you need to learn to walk gently, quietly, for you are so … like the wind," Ovanes laughed involuntarily, touched Hrisoula's shoulder and she was embarrassed, "Well, I know, I'll do whatever you say."

With the kittens, they settled in a small room behind the staircase. The two beds there shone with the whiteness of the bedspreads. "We could fall from them, look how high they are," Pinyo was fretting. A transparent curtain was hanging in neat folds and through it, one could see the backyard with piles of firewood, carefully arranged in a tall shed. Hrisoula raised a warning finger, "Watch out! We had good luck, you see, found a wealthy home, now we shouldn't do anything wrong, or … Work doesn't scare me, but that Ovanes, I don't know …" "Why, he's a good man," Pinyo objected, "a little curmudgeonly, though, but if this is his only fault …" Hrisoula poked the dimple on her chin. "Oh, you, as if you knew anything about men!"

One evening Syruie told them she wanted the kittens, so Pinyo took them up in the basket. The light of a big gas lamp on the wall stretched their shadows. The guest sat on the edge of the chair and folded her scratched tanned legs under it. Everything here also sparkled with cleanliness and that neatness in the house worried her.

Syruie played timidly with the kittens; one of them scratched her and she cried, not from the pain, but rather, anger. She gestured that she wanted Pinyo to put them back in the basket and the girl started chasing them around the room. Sitting in the bed with her chin on her knees, Syruie was watching the fuss. At last, Pinyo soothed the kittens, threw the loosely knit headscarf on top of the basket, and tied it with an elastic band. She sat on the chair pressing the basket against her chest and did not dare stir. Finally, Syruie spoke,

"Why animals have nails is clear to me, but why people have them is not."

And she sent Pinyo away.

Content, Pinyo climbed down the stairs, how nice Syruie doesn't want me! … She prances lightly and looks closely at her image in every mirror: she has certainly fleshed out, she has, her hair's soft from the soap and warm water, her cheeks shine like apples, she wears a green skirt and scarlet slippers—she likes her new self so much. Hrisoula's transformation is even bigger, wow, how beautiful she is in the blue skirt and yellow slippers she wears, despite Ovanes' warning, "In this town, lass, only Turkish women wear yellow slippers, Christian women are not allowed." Hrisoula tossed her head, "I want yellow slippers," and for some inexplicable reason, Ovanes did not object and after measuring their feet, he went to the bazar in the town center and bought the slippers and oh, how they mince their steps now in these slippers, how cheerfully they stomp the earth.

She had just come back home when Ovanes knocked on their door. Syruie wanted Pinyo to sleep with her but she should go without the kittens. Pinyo left the basket with Hrisoula, and reluctantly climbed back. Behind her, Ovanes switched off all the lamps and withdrew to his room. It was dark, she wanted to sleep and hurriedly curled on the floor by the bed but Syruie ordered her sternly to climb into the bed and lie with her head to the girl's feet, the way Syrui's mother had slept with a friend in her childhood, staying awake till late and sharing secrets. Obediently, Pinyo climbed into the bed, curled up like a kitten and was about to fall asleep fast because there was nothing to share, really, but Ovanes' girl chased her sleep away, "Don't fall asleep, I'll show you something tonight!"

She kept silent for a little while and then spoke in a clear, stern voice,

"Tonight, I'll show you my mother!"

Pinyo winced.

"Don't say anything," Syruie said sharply, "Every Sunday my mother comes to see me from there. Look, I've left the window open. You just keep quiet, don't make a sound whatever you see."

Pinyo bit her lips. She'd grown up in nature where everything could be seen, smelled, touched because it existed in there, perfectly normal and real. This girl was talking about things that scared her. Ten years ago, Syruie's mother had died at birth and the girl must be dreaming about her now, a glassy head like hers cannot but dream of something like this.

She comes and she is all silver.

Her love feels stronger because I've missed her.

Everything in this world turns into another when the time comes; only love does not turn into anything else; it's always love.

Syruie fell asleep, and started breathing rhythmically. Pinyo lay awake and sleep overcame her at about midnight. She was just dozing off when very clearly, she heard the girl's words,

"Oh, Mom! I see you!"

Pinyo jumped up and sat in her bed. The curtain softly

yielded and a faint whiff like a velvet tail twisted above their heads. A pulsing thread of thin blue light circled around the girl's head and drained through the pillow, "Did you see how beautiful she is, Pinyo, how silver!" Pinyo hesitantly muttered something.

"You are blind then! I thought you could see, but you are like everybody else!"

Syruie turned her angry face to the wall and soon was breathing evenly. Lying at her feet, Pinyo was thinking how Syruie's talk was strange as if she were some white-haired old lady. Frightened, she sneaked out of the room and tiptoed back to Hrisoula. Once in bed, she fell asleep right away.

Fall was near and the yard smelled of dry basil, bitter marigolds and mums. Hrisoula drops into her bosom the bitter marigold leaves; smells of fall too. She wakes up early, spends a long time trying to wake up Pinyo, pulls her out of the blankets and grumbles, "So easy to get used to the featherbed, princess, so easy to forget the straw mat!" The girl whimpers pitifully. "Try not to get spoiled, little girl, because your soul in a spoiled body would look just like the thistle Irinyo's put in a crystal vase. You know, the soul needs a proper container, is that right!" Irinyo was the family's old cook; Hrisoula and she did not like each other from the start and each spoke of the other with dislike. "Ha, what's wrong with the thistle in this vase; looks pretty nice to me," the girl teased. Hrisoula raved, "Look who's talking! As if you understood anything, like Irinyo! You should know, Pinyo, that God has arranged things in this world and nobody should mess it up! And what is ugly should not mesh with the beautiful; God will think of another reward instead for not doing a good job on looks!" But Hrisoula suddenly doubts her philosophy, "Sometimes you can't tell one from the other, though; what for some is beautiful, for others is ugly as sin, if you know what I mean! She proudly sticks her chest out: nothing to explain, really, just look at me dark and ugly, yes, but ain't I beautiful?" Both stare at each other, start giggling together and tussle on the messy bed.

Today, Hrisoula put on her blue skirt, smoothed the curls on her forehead with some spit so they wouldn't stick out like metal turnings, smoothed her eyebrows and looked at herself in the mirror,

"The feast begins!"

They were about to light the furnace for the first time this fall and Ovanes had ordered them to put on brand new clothes. "The glaziers have followed this custom since olden times, girls; the Assyrians and Babylonians even recorded it on some baked clay tiles: on the day the furnace is ignited, all who work around it should put on clean clothes and make a sacrifice to the gods ..." and Ovanes bought them new skirts at the bazaar. The girls put them on and tried all the mirrors in the house. "Wow, I look at myself and I envy my own image!" Hrisoula combed Pinyo's hair with the ox horn comb, rubbed her cheeks with a wet towel so they shone like they were polished, and solemnly led her to the furnace, "In my life, I have never prepared for anything in advance; everything has happened by itself, but now, look how long we have waited for this celebration! You see, Pinyo, the waiting makes the feast longer. I'd even wait a little longer—I don't want it to start, for once it starts, it will soon be over."

Ovanes was at the furnace, dressed in his French clothes—he had spent his childhood and youth in Marseilles. He was waiting patiently, "I see you've done a good job dressing up …" he smiled faintly, "I wonder if people understand that the meaning of life is in their work! It's too simple to comprehend! …" His excitement was obvious. He was rumbling in lower tones than usual, stomping the earth like a bear, rubbing his hands and biting his lips.

"Do people understand that the purpose of life is in doing something that gives pleasure?"

The Armenian made Hrisoula walk with burning incense around the furnace. Then he got down to work: he mixed the sand and limestone, added the soda in portions, stirred and Hrisoula was pouring from that mixture in the clay pot. Finally the man lit the fire.

Pinyo's squatting beside them, enjoying the fuss. At last, something new in this house, whose unchanging routine had started to bore her: all day long shaking the carpets, dusting, polishing the furniture and not showing their noses outside, for a few weeks now. Syruie is quiet and angry at the girl, who looks but does not see, and as quietly, Pinyo yearns for the life they lost. She misses the wood, the sun, the evergreen prickly bushes—there, freedom felt like a soap bubble inside her; here, her body's heavy like it were filled with lead. She is even getting clumsier, knocking cups and vases around; Hrisoula secretly gathers the pieces, throws them away and scolds her," What is wrong with you! …"One day the girl tried to explain, "I feel in a cage, that's what!" Hrisoula sneered, "Aha, the little wild beast lost its freedom! How come, huh, Pinyo?" Pinyo snarled at her, "Because of you, we ran away from freedom!"

Hrisoula was suddenly serious,

"Look at me, Pinyo, have I changed?"

It was strange, but Hrisoula hadn't changed a lot. She ran around the house like the wind, sang with her husky voice, filled her bosom with the leaves of the late-blooming marigolds, giggled for no obvious reason and did her work quickly. Pinyo had to admit that she hadn't changed, only the skirt she wore made her look tamer. "You see," Hrisoula said, "I haven't changed because freedom is in me, I haven't lost it. Freedom is not outside, but inside. Is that right, girl? Nobody else understands freedom better than us, yes, we may be simple-minded and ignorant, but we understand freedom at least as much as the butterflies and ladybugs do! So, remember this from me: each of us is responsible for our own freedom and it's up to us to lose it or not."

Hrisoula left Pinyo alone and went on to dust the mirrors, admire her image and whistle loudly.

Now, she is sitting at the furnace and Pinyo sees how serious she is: her cheeks are burning, her eyes sparkling as she's thinking about something and staring at the crimson tongues of the fire. Ovanes looks at her from under his eyebrows but says nothing. Recently, he's taken to looking secretly at her, before leaving with a sigh. Today Hrisoula stares at the fire as if hypnotized and as if hypnotized, Ovanes looks at her. Pinyo looks at both, livid.

In the evening she spilled the beans,

"Ovanes looks at you like you were the moon!"

Hrisoula just sighed.

She took turns with Ovanes to keep the fire burning while the mixture was melting. It was a long and tiresome process: the melting had to be repeated in long flat pots, the fire needed to be kept at a certain temperature, the furnace required somebody around at all times. The idea that the thing can happen between the Armenian and Hrisoula flashed through Pinyo's mind and she froze in terror. They had gone through too much trouble together because of it; she should not allow this to happen again, not for the world! When Hrisoula got up at night and put on her shoes, she sneaked after her.

But nothing happened. The man let Hrisoula sit on the three-legged stool, gave instructions and left. Pinyo stayed a while behind the sand sack and also left.

Work was going well. The Armenian was content that the glass was melting with no foam, stones or bubbles. "Marvelous vessels will come out of this," Irinyo's shrill voice was heard when everybody gathered at a distance to watch the noisily bubbling mixture. Irinyo started whining,

"Oh, what a pity the mistress is not alive! She wanted a rainbow colored lamp so much! Now, this glass here may turn into something like it!"

Dismayed, Ovanes looked at her,

"How do you know?"

"Mistress Elenitsa told me herself, well before her skin dried like a snake's from that thing … love, you know," Irinyo blurted out without batting an eye.

Ovanes raged at her. What is she talking about, what snake, she should go to the kitchen and never show her nose here. The cook, offended, flipped her skirts: "I know everything. What are my eyes for if they don't see what's going on in this house!"

Pinyo was shaken up. Like a snake's skin! She quietly

followed the cook into the kitchen, where she was clanking pots and spoons around to overcome her anger.

"Tell me about mistress Elenitsa!"

But Irinyo knew nothing now, she could tell nothing, and mistress Elenitsa was not here anymore … "Well, she was sweet, honey sweet, and when the master carried her in his arms, she was shining like the moon … he's dark, you know, and she, golden—they were born for each other, and their bed sang every night."

Irinyo slammed a lid on a pot, "Go away and don't stick your nose in here, he says, but only I know how he took the life out of her, the poor thing."

Pinyo's eyes widened.

"He did?! How?"

"With his love, that's how!"

"Irinyo!"

"His love sucked her strength, and she just melted! In the end she left her body and vanished into thin air, that's how! Only her golden skin was left on the bed, like a snake's, there! One night, soon after her death, the door to their bedroom was ajar and I peeked in: the master was asleep and something shone on one side of the bed and sparkled in the moonlight! Honest to God!"

Her face sallow with fear, Pinyo hardly managed to whisper,

"But how, Irinyo, how did his love suck her life out?!"

"How? This is how! How can a man suck the life out of a young, frail mistress? Especially, a bear of a man like our master …"

"But … but he said she died giving birth to Syruie!"

"Yes, but only it was two months later. You'd think he can't say boo to a goose but if he grabs a woman, her bones crack like she were a sparrow!"

"But why would he grab her? Why, huh, why Irinyo?!"

The cook saw the shock in the girl's eyes and came to her senses. What was she doing talking to this wild one, a child into the bargain! She was just hurt, so she thought this up. Go straight to the kitchen and don't show your nose out?! How does he dare, the black Armenian! But Irinyo knows better!

One day Syruie wanted to see the kittens again. She was sitting in bed and her big head was shining in the sunlight like an orange cloud. A strange scent was in the room and teased Pinyo's little beast's sense of smell. It was like pine honey had melted in the air, mixed with the scent of Greek gum and something else, elusive, tender and soft. "Did your mother come, Syruie!" *Mistress Elenitsa was gentle and honey sweet.* "Was that your mother came last night?" Syruie squinted her eyes, "I don't know what you mean. Give me the kittens now."

But Pinyo was sure now, mistress Elenitsa had been in this room. Recently, she had developed a new, complex sense of smell and could distinguish people by their specific smell: *several times a day for the last few weeks, I've walked out to the street, curiously observing the passersby. Their smell tells me about their characters: breathing in, my nostrils recognize some faint, specific scents floating in the air—how come the other people don't smell those? Hrisoula is cross with me; enough with all that craziness, you …*

This new sensibility Pinyo developed very quickly, but it could have been always with her and just sprouting right now, like a pale green, fresh stalk piercing the soil from the onion bulb.

The girl nonchalantly ignored Hrisoula's fear that this could be one of God's gifts: it's not easy to know that somebody else, and not just anybody at that, orders your nose about … "But why do you need all this, Pinyo?" The girl, though, was having fun and soon started to recognize the innermost character features of different passersby. Some men and women had the heavy, intoxicating smell of the hot Arab Levanto. She would instinctively stay away from them—they were secretive, sensual, mean, unpredictable; she could not find exact words to describe their aura, but she did not doubt her senses. Others gave off a fresh breath of juniper and hay, and they were the ones she'd always trust: they were simple, of few words, hearty. Then there were others who smelled of bread and milk wheat, and they were the most generous people, but rarely met. All kinds of body scents existed and for weeks on end, from morning till night, Pinyo was on the street, testing her new gift with joy.

When she told Hrisoula how exactly she distinguished among the different bodies' emanations, Hrisoula squinted her eyes, "What do I smell of?" Pinyo laughed, "You smell of geranium, wild rose, thyme, violets, wind— of all the wood together! It's true, Hrisoula, you smell of the woods!" Now Hrisoula laughed. "How about Irinyo?" The girl started jumping in place, "Gee, looking at her, Hrisoula, what do you think she smells of? She is an olive in vinegar and oil, that's her smell!"

Hrisoula didn't even smile.

"How about Ovanes, what does he smell of?"

Pinyo was quiet.

"Come on, tell me!"

"He is a good man," the girl answered seriously,

"because he smells of sadness."

So this explains why now Pinyo was sure it was mistress Elenitsa who left this sweet, elusive scent in Syruie's room. Ovanes' daughter kept her alienated silence, and Pinyo could hardly stand her sullen mood: staring fixedly at the ceiling, her eyes always gloomy but her hair ginger, pathetically soft and fluffy like a baby's. Watching the sunset now, Syruie spoke, "Do you know where the sun goes in the evening?"

Pinyo was quick to answer, "Behind the hills; where else could it go? I've seen that in the mountains many times!"

"You are wrong."

"So what?"

"Making mistakes is good, sometimes."

Pinyo wanted to leave the room, but Syruie fixed her heavy glance on her. "Don't rush!" She hugged her knees and was quiet for a long time. Then, suddenly her impossible voice piped up, "Do you know what the sun is, huh, Pinyo?" The girl is impatient, "A fireplace with fire burning in it. Hrisoula told me."

Syruie muttered something contemptuously. The sun was love, all the love in the world was up there, hasn't it ever crossed Despinyo's mind, and that was why billions of sunbeams shone upon the earth every day, one for each person, their own private sunbeams.

Syruie looks stern, like a white-haired old lady, "They are the love that God gives to the people, as much as each can bear!"

"Yes, but we can't see God, Syruie. What are you talking about? God is invisible to the eye, and his love too, along with many other things."

"Nothing is invisible. Each thing can be seen, even the invisible if you have the eyes for it."

"But, of course, I have eyes!"

"You don't need eyes to see this, foolish Pinyo. Stop bothering me, how is it possible for the eyes to see the invisible!"

"But you said …"

"I didn't say this. I just said that invisible things don't exist, but you don't understand. You better go away."

"Love, hate, bla-bla," Pinyo was running down the stairs. "What do I care! She'd do better to love me visibly, instead of just going bla-bla. She should love Hrisoula too, not despise us …"

It was obvious, though, that Syruie talked like that even with her father—her tone was patronizing and bored as if he were the child, and she—the parent. Strange thoughts, not of a child, were born in her glass head, but we all around her were busy with urgent routines: cooking, helping Ovanes at the furnace, laughing, chattering, singing. We had no time for thinking—we just exuded our lives' scents and lived as we knew.

The weird thing was that only Syruie did not have any scent.

Ceremoniously, Ovanes brings into the room a big gas lamp. He carries it carefully in his arms, places it on the small, tall table, puts his hands on his waist and silently stares at it. Behind him, everybody watches. The lamp's shade has the colors of the rainbow. Irinyo claps her hands and speaks quickly,

"Ah, master, how happy mistress Elenitsa would be if she were alive! Ah, master! You've made it for her!"

"Shut up!" Ovanes interrupted her.

And in order to hide the excitement swelling in his

chest, he started explaining hurriedly,

"To make colorful glass, it is very important to dose the dyes right. This, bright yellow color is called Neapolitan yellow. You mix lead and antimony and what you get is Neapolitan yellow. It's like the sun! For the red and blue, on the other hand, you need copper oxide. It's simple, but the dosage is important."

Syruie arrives and watches silently. Then she approaches and runs her finger on the glass. She turns and they see her sparkling eyes, drowned in tears. She suddenly buries her face in her father's chest and cries out, her voice thin and dismal like a kitten's. Ovanes starts to calm her down and leads her up the stairs.

Then Pinyo notices that when Hrisoula is dusting, she spends a lot of time thinking, with the duster on the shade of the new lamp. "I don't like it at all, though, it's too beautiful." Hrisoula winks at her, "Mistress Elenitsa was very beautiful too, and that's what I don't like."

What is she talking about?!

Pinyo started to spy on Hrisoula again. She was sure that the glass shade, this sparkling provocation, would poke her eyes and push her back to do something reckless very soon. It happened right before her shocked eyes and she could do nothing to prevent it.

It was midnight and Hrisoula was late again. Pinyo jumped out of bed and without even putting her slippers on, walked barefoot through the house, crossed the cobbled yard, slid like a cat against the wall and peeked in.

They stand as if frozen, facing each other and looking in each other's eyes. The fire casts shadows on the walls, Hrisoula's eyes sparkle, her Karakachan blood makes her cheeks burn. And here, Ovanes slowly raises his hand

and places it on her hair, caressing it very gently; then his palm moves down caressing her back; he picks her up from under the hips, buries his face in her breasts, and she wraps her arms around his neck.

They stand like this and the fire lights them up.

Ovanes let go of the girl, touched her face with the back of his hand, uttered something. Hrisoula bent her head and the light in her eyes died. She headed for the door and Pinyo dashed on tiptoes to go back before her.

The following evening Hrisoula's footsteps passed by their door, climbed up the steps and sunk in the carpets upstairs. Ovanes' slow, heavy steps passed by shortly after.

Pinyo sprang up, her heart beating madly. This time, she wouldn't allow it. She wouldn't allow it for the world! Hrisoula's madness to do that thing with men would cause new problems for them both. She tiptoed upstairs and stood in front of Ovanes' door. She was cautious although she had decided to intervene right away. She told herself that first she must find out what exactly was going on.

She opened the door just a crack.

The two of them were stark naked. Hrisoula—thin and fragile, her hair tousled like a thick bush. Ovanes— big and strong, like a giant. The fire was burning in the fireplace and in the corner, the new lamp was shining brightly.

Like a real rainbow! Wow! This must have been Hrisoula's idea. She was facing the myth of mistress Elenitsa; she wanted to fight with it, tear it to pieces.

I, Pinyo, just stood there and stared meekly. Ovanes made a step back to turn down the fuse and then I saw something that stunned me. I had seen the donkeys in the mountains, but never thought of why they are like this sometimes. Now I understood and wanted to leave but had no strength. Shocked, I just kept on watching.

Ovanes was pressing against her, caressing her tenderly, his hands all over her body. His lips drank her skin. Breathless and tender, he was whispering something and Hrisoula was silent, giving in to him. Lifting her gently, Ovanes put her on the bed and lay on top of her. On the white sheet, their tangled dark bodies looked like a huge octopus.

The man pushed violently, just like Yorgos before; Hrisoula tilted her head backwards and the whites of her eyes showed through her half-closed eyelids.

Pinyo came to her senses.

Pressing a hand on her mouth, she tiptoed downstairs and slid shaking into her bed. She tried to fall asleep, but kept seeing Ovanes, his dark naked body and that thing, hard and stretched tight, which could not but frighten the child Pinyo actually was.

It seemed she now knew everything.

The next day, Syruie stopped in the middle of the hall, her head swaying on her skinny neck, and stared heavily into her father's eyes,

"Where's Mom's lamp?"

Ovanes was confused. "It may break by chance, so …" He took it up to his room to keep it safe. Syruie did not say anything else. She just fixed her heavy glance on Hrisoula, turned around and wobbled up the stairs.

Pinyo closed her eyes tight and saw again how Ovanes was drinking Hrisoula's skin and remembered Irinyo's words, *he dried her up, he sucked her in.* She was worried about Hrisoula. Her anxious eyes followed her everywhere and she worried that Hrisoula had changed: her body had gotten even thinner, her cheekbones more prominent, her eyes bigger and their sparkle more restless.

I'll tell her we should run.

Ovanes started melting a special kind of glass. "Optical, they call it," he explained briefly. Anyway, they understood nothing but remembered that the mixture should be stirred with clay sticks so that no bubbles appeared and a certain dosage of boric acid should be added. The man and Hrisoula still took turns in keeping the fire up. Sometimes she'd come home right away after her turn, sometimes she'd come back right before dawn. She had become unusually quiet and reserved. She stirred the mixture, kept the fire up, arranged the crucibles, even tried to blow a glass with the blower, but it came out lopsided and squat though Ovanes liked it very much and took it to his room. Hrisoula was working as always but it was obvious that something was bothering her.

Finally, the mixture was ready and Ovanes poured the optical glass. "I'll make lenses, thicker than Irinyo's thickest plates." The mixture cooled and he started polishing the lenses. "What do you need this for?" Hrisoula ventured and Ovanes beamed,

"I'll make a telescope. I want to see God in heaven!"

They thought he was joking. Excited, he told them about some Galileo Galilei, the first in the world to make a telescope with lenses that magnified the objects 32 times; so this Galilei placed the tube on a tower in Venice, pointed it towards the stars and then he saw a miracle unseen: The Milky Way, which people thought was white milk formed by vapors, wasn't like that at all but just billions of sparkling stars, invisible to the naked eye. "Well, no," objected Hrisoula and Pinyo, "this is the

Straw spilled in the field of the sky."

Syruie entered and listened.

"The sky is something with no beginning or end, girls, but how many people ever think of looking up. It's full of billions of stars, suns, nebulas. Up there somewhere is God, who created this infinite world and I, Ovanes the glazier, will make lenses to enlarge things 100 times, and I'll look for God in the celestial altitudes. And I'll show him to you!"

Pinyo interrupted timidly, "Tell us about God, Ovanes."

It was true, she had heard about him, but she felt quite scared of this sour white-bearded old man sitting up there on a cloud with nothing to do but spy on what this skinny mischief Despina was doing—the same Pina that the Karakachans in the mountains constantly scolded, "God will punish you, Pinyo, he will cut your ears, what have you done again?"

Ovanes put his hand on her shoulder,

"God is the Great Creator of all things alive and not alive. He is the Master Artist."

Then Syruie's thin challenging voice interrupted,

"If he is the Great Creator, his creations should be great, right? But just look around! He made some people that are not like anything! Like your faulty glasses."

"Don't be blasphemous!"

Syruie laughs, Syruie's rolling on the floor laughing. Why, doesn't Ovanes, the glazier, see what people are really like: they lie, steal, kill, they are born with heads like water jugs or lame and crippled. Why had God created them like this if he was such a great master!

Ovanes scowled. It's not God that created them so, but

they turned out so because they wanted to. God had given them free will, the opportunity to choose their behavior in life. Disabilities were something else, something with a deep cause; otherwise, all the babies were born good and innocent.

"Who told you that, glazier? The babies are born helpless, that's what I know."

"Choice is a sacred human right, but people are born equally innocent."

"It's not true. We are born with sins, even before we have committed them!"

"This is because of the Fall."

"But what is the Fall, Ovanes? Eve ate the apple and knew the truth. She knew the truth and made Adam grasp it, too, and they were punished for knowing the truth. What could be that truth that God so jealously hides from his creations, huh, dad?"

Ovanes shook his head helplessly. Syruie changed the topic,

"Why do you want to see God?"

"I want to see him with my own eyes. I'll be the first to have seen God with my own eyes!"

Syruie, who until this moment was teasing reluctantly and calmly, suddenly tried to spring to her feet. Her head swayed on her thin neck,

"If you can't see God with your eyes closed, Ovanes, even if your telescope can enlarge things 1000 times, you still won't catch a glimpse of him. Just give up!"

"Indeed!"

"The telescope is nothing but an eye. Much more powerful, but still an eye, right? And God is invisible to the eyes."

"We'll find out if this is so."

"Look at you, Doubting Thomas! Do you believe in God or not?"

"Of course I do and you know it!"

"Then why do you need to look into something you believe in? Faith is not verifiable, Ovanes, because it turns into no faith!"

Silence fell. Syruie picked up the edge of her scarlet skirt, swung around and left walking carefully as if afraid the wind could blow her away. She crossed the frosty yard and entered the house without turning back though she probably felt their looks on her back.

Ovanes hid the thick glass and gave up on the telescope.

I sense that Ovanes has absorbed much of Hrisoula's scent and exudes it himself.

"I know what you are doing with Ovanes."

Silence.

"I already know everything."

Hrisoula rubs her brow, her eyes bulging,

"You don't know anything."

"You did the same with Yorgos.'

"It's not the same at all. Not at all, Despinyo!"

Bristling, the girl waits,

"You are not little anymore, soon you'll be a woman. You should know some things. I thought I should prepare you, but I see that you are not wasting your time and have picked up things on your own … always following me! You misunderstood, though …"

"Tell me then! Tell me!"

Pinyo recalls Yorgos' wild moaning as his tongue was picking the petals from Hrisoula's bosom. She recalls Ovanes gently sucking Hrisoula's skin, all her naked body.

"What you've seen, I don't know how it looks from aside, but it's not a bad thing. Ovanes told me that God had made a mold first and in this mold he'd shaped the man from mud, and from the man's rib, the woman. Only one man and one woman. Then he broke the mold. In an infinite number of molds, he created the men and women, and, as I see it at least, he then chased them away to wander in the wide world, to seek and find each other. If they could, that is! God frowned at them for the apple, the one the first lovers stole, and he banished them. So now the man seeks the woman and the woman seeks the man, so they can unite into a whole, like the mold made them. You see? And now I'll give you a piece of my mind because I saw you stealing apples from the neighbor's late blooming apple tree! ... Whatever else you want, a cherry, morello, pear ... you can pick, I know you fancy them, but don't touch the apples. They call them the forbidden fruit! God sees everything.."

"God again! What is he doing, really!"

"But Hrisoula, I worry that Ovanes could suck your life out of you and only your dark skin will remain! It'll shed in the bed like a snake's!"

"Don't listen to Irinyo's babble, she's just a bird-brain."

"Yes, but she told me about mistress Elenitsa and ..."

"Mistress Elenitsa again! Aren't I better looking, Despinyo? Look, aren't I better?"

So alive is the glazier' dead wife in Pinyo's imagination that she can see them next to each other and compare right away the sweet, golden Elenitsa with her velvet eyes and the reckless, whirlwind Hrisoula, her olive skin and high cheek bones, lit by the azure glance, her thick, sharp hair and low husky voice.

"Well, you have no equal!"

She throws her arms around her neck, gives her a hot kiss on the cheek and content, Hrisoula beams.

After that talk, Pinyo fell easily asleep and did not strain to hear Hrisoula coming back home at night. She was not worried about her anymore. She was just wondering whether Ovanes or Yorgos was the only one for Hrisoula, her other half in God's mold. She'd said, *it's not at all the same as with Yorgos.*

One night in the beginning of winter, a blizzard was raging outside. Dogs were howling, doors were slamming, snow was pouring down. The night was stormy and restless. Hrisoula was not in the room; she had not come back after her turn at the furnace. Despite the storm, Pinyo drifted into sleep. After a while she felt a hand shaking her shoulder. Syruie, bent over her head, was shivering in her nightgown,

"Where's Hrisoula?"

She suddenly turned around and headed for the door wobbling as if she was sinking in holes.

"Syruie, go to your room, you'll freeze and get sick! Let me take you to your room, and if you want I can stay with you. Let's go Syruinyo!"

Pinyo fawns over her, frozen with fear, but Syruie is already on her way to Ovanes' door. Pinyo catches up with her and pulls at her nightgown, but Syruie slips away and pushes the handle.

The blizzard prevented them from hearing and the girls saw them. Like a shining flower, the colorful lamp lit up the bed in which Ovanes' lips drank Hrisoula's breasts. They clung to each other—two halves of a whole; the man and the woman had found each other and would never be alone.

Syruie squealed like a chicken and collapsed. Pinyo rushed down the stairs and into her bed. She closed her eyes tight and stopped her ears, not to see and hear what else was about to happen.

What happened was that Syruie shut up and froze like a stone: just sits stiff in her bed, doesn't eat or drink, only her glass head gets bigger, hardly balancing on her long, skinny neck. She didn't let anybody in. In vain did her father keep watch at her door, walking to and fro with heavy strides. Irinyo also tried to enter but Syruie's glance sent her back. Pinyo would peek in every now and then, hugging one of the kittens, but the girl did not notice her either. They saw her melting in front of their eyes, small and serious, thin pale lips tightly pressed together, but they could do nothing. Hrisoula and Ovanes avoided looking at each other. The cook in the kitchen was slamming lids around and pouring hot curses.

One day, Syruie saw Pinyo peeking in and lifted her thin yellow hand to call her in. Hesitantly, the girl stepped inside and gave her the basket. The kittens scrambled out and started licking Syruie's hands.

"I guessed about that thing because mom stopped coming. As long as Hrisoula lives in this house, my mom won't ever come again."

She played with the kittens but did not see them.

"Sometimes I think I'm a hundred years old. I must be that old; I feel time flows differently through me. I'm very old, Pinyo!"

"You are only two years older than me, Syruie …"

"Ancient is what I am, ancient!"

Only I knew her deeply cherished secret; I had inhaled

once the sweet scent of something invisible, but shocking as perception. I decided to tell Ovanes.

Ovanes listened to what Pinyo had to say and his gloomy eyes sparkled, "I'll make the telescope! I got the blueprints of the device and some parts cousin Bedros sent me from Marseilles!"

So he started making the telescope. He polished the thick glass again to make two lenses out of it, convex and concave so they could start magnifying 100 times and the sick Syruie could see her mother in heaven and stop longing for her. It never crossed his mind that there was an easier way to cure his daughter—by throwing the two girls out of the house.

Ovanes finished the telescope one night in the middle of winter. He never left his shop until he finished; his meals were brought to him, but he did not eat right—he lost weight, his nose looked longer, his eyes had a feverish glow. When finally he attached the device to the tube, he tossed back his head, clasped his hands behind his neck and stood like that for a long time. Was he praying to his God or to Mistress Elenitsa? His feelings passed across his face like the shadows of clouds … Then he stood up, gingerly picked up the tube and entered the house.

He came back crestfallen and slammed the wall with his fist. "There's no telescope for the souls, that's what she said. Go to her, Pinyo, she is waiting for you."

Syruie had lost so much weight that she was just one swollen, now really transparent head. She was sitting in bed and the telescope was set up on the window sill. Not knowing what to say, Pinyo just sat down. Syruie looked at her with eyes distant and cold as ice,

"Look at the stars if you want; they are really

beautiful.”

“But … there’s no stars tonight, the sky’s dark!”

“Try, just try.”

Pinyo stood at the tube, looked and, scared, stepped back—a huge sky stretched in front; she bumped into it and sank there. Big and bright were the stars. Scary. She stepped away from the tube, the sky vanished, and she suddenly felt small and insignificant.

“Why were you scared? You don’t know, do you? You saw perfection, that’s why, Despinyo. My father always repeats God, perfection, but he can’t understand that beauty could be as scary as ugliness. If a man can’t bear it, it is dangerous for him.”

I had the same feeling when Hrisoula piled flowers and herbs in my cradle.

“God is really there, in all mind-boggling things like what you just saw through the telescope. But why should my father search for God among the stars if he hadn’t realized that God is in a thousand places and in a thousand things—he is not in one place, he has a little bitty part of him everywhere. In all the stars, in each person.”

“In me, too?”

“In you, too, Despinyo, don’t you feel it? When you are good and happy, you can’t contain yourself. You get bigger like something blows you up from the inside.”

“That’s right!”

They were quiet. The wind was blowing and they listened to its howl. After some time Syruie leaned over and whispered in Pinyo’s ear,

“Hrisoula’s dangerous beauty weighs down on my father and he has no strength to bear it. He is not ready for her!”

"Then why ... Why don't you throw us out, Hrisoula and me?"

"Because, Pinyo, beauty can kill from a distance as well, even more securely. Leave me alone now, I am tired."

Judging by her words, with every passing minute Syruie was getting years older. This scared Pinyo and she started to avoid her.

Ovanes called a doctor, a Frenchman with a thin mustache and raven hair, smoothed with vaseline.

"The girl has hydrocephalus, right? It's a miracle she's still alive; even through the skull, it's clear how the brain has all turned into water! I wonder how come she's conscious, you see? What is more, somehow she thinks," the Frenchman spoke indifferently, not in the least aware of his cruelty. On his way out, he brushed the snow from a maroon chrysanthemum, miraculously survived, plucked it off and thrust it in his buttonhole.

Ovanes locked himself in his room. Hrisoula lay curled up on her bed. Only Pinyo was running up and down—now to Syruie, now to Hrisoula.

One day, Syruie unexpectedly asked about her father and Pinyo told her. "Poor dad," muttered Syruie, "go tell him that I saw mom last night, through the telescope. Tell him I ask him to come see me."

Ovanes burst into tears and wiping them with his sleeve walked to his daughter's room like a bear. At the door, he lingered for a while, then hesitantly opened it and stood on the doorstep.

"Come in, daddy, don't be afraid."

Later both stepped out, their faces lit up with the light of mutual forgiveness. Syruie went to Hrisoula, who was dusting the furniture, and touched her hand. Scared,

Hrisoula shuddered and froze.

"You are not to blame; just learn to control your beauty for it's like the blizzard outside!"

Then she entered the kitchen and asked for pancakes with plum jam. Irinyo hovered around, pans and pots were clanking, it smelled of fried dough. Syruie called Pinyo to share the pancakes and nibbling like a kitten, she said,

"I lied about seeing mom through the telescope. But, tonight she's sure to come because … it's Saturday."

Hrisoula was waiting in her room downstairs. She stood at the window, holding the lace curtain with two fingers and peeking at the dazzling white snow. It was a truly beautiful sight: a dark girl on the background of the sparkling snow. She sensed Pinyo's presence and shuddered but remained with her back to her. "Sit down, I want to tell you something!"

They left the basket with the kittens with Irinyo so Syruie could play with them when she felt like it. The cook took the basket and pretended she did not understand anything. She neither asked where they were going nor did they tell her. Ovanes was not at home and that was good according to Hrisoula, so as *not to make him feel uncomfortable in trying to stop us while he actually wants us to leave!*

"We are running away again," Pinyo commented.

Hrisoula did not reply.

They stayed with Vassilaki, the furrier, until midsummer. He had agreed to take them in without the kittens. He lived alone, never had a wife or another living creature with him and he spent his whole day in his shop on the main street while his two apprentices cut and sewed in the workshop at the end of the narrow yard, where they also lived. They were two Albanian boys, brothers, blondish and pale-eyed, black fezzes on their heads. Esad, always smiling and sipping from a small flask, whistled from morning till night; the younger, Effy, had a bad stutter and preferred to keep quiet. Here again, Hrisoula and Pinyo dusted, washed, cleaned until noon and in the afternoon worked in a room filled to the ceiling with uncarded wool. Tens of kilograms of wool passed through their hands: they carded it with their fingers, cleaned the burs and thorns, carded again, until the wool turned into a fluffy voluminous cloud. Then they filled the wool in sacks and arranged them by the wall. In the evening they sat with the master to eat stew or lentil soup. They went to bed early and got up early and worked a lot although they'd agreed to work just enough for food.

Spring stole in quietly and Hrisoula picked the first rose from the garden, dropped the petals in her bosom, looked at the blue sky and smiled, "You see, Pinyo, the sky really has no end. Come summer, my girl, we'll just leave and walk without direction under this sky. If something's moving inside a man, how can he stop himself! We could go as far as Italy to see that Galilengalilen in Venice, what do you say?"

She had made up her mind that they head for some other town, like Chorlu or Rodosto: she just liked their names. Her nomadic blood was calling; she couldn't sit still. In Ovanes' house, such thoughts would never cross her mind. Pinyo was trying to understand if she was still pining after the Armenian because she seemed to have forgotten him. She remembered the tender mist swimming in her eyes when she was sitting in the cabin longing for Yorgos. Ovanes did not seem to be on her mind anymore. Then why did she let him fondle her and lie in the same bed with her? After the conversation they had then, Pinyo did not feel embarrassed anymore and one day she asked her flat out, "You don't miss Ovanes! I remember how you missed Yorgos but you don't care for Ovanes anymore. Then why did you let him take off your clothes; why did you do that thing? He's not your other half, the one from the mold, right?"

Hrisoula clapped her hands. All that pile of wool to the ceiling was waiting for them and some people still had their heads in the clouds! She flicked Pinyo's nose with her fingers, pushed her in the soft wool and started tickling her. Pinyo tore herself away,

"You have no shame, Hrisoula! You want to be with all the men in the world!"

Then Hrisoula chased her out.

She roamed the neighborhood until dusk, went down to the river with the copper pot and caught fish in the water seething with white fish, went back and cooked soup. Only then did Hrisoula relent. "Listen, my girl, and remember because you were born a woman and you need to know from now on. The man God made in one mold with you is the only one for you, it goes without saying. You might not find him in this life at all. What if he lives in another country like that Marseilles or Venice, huh? How will you find him, the one and only man, Pinyo, if he lives at the end of the world? You only hope that everything is in the hands of fate, but is that really so? Look what Yorgos did. Why couldn't he wait for me to grow up, but married my sister, Katerina, gave me a gold coin at the wedding and spanked my skinny ass. He had no idea whatsoever that I was his half! We lived in the same mountain, rubbed shoulders every day—fate had tried and outdone itself, but there! If he'd known I was his only one, would he have waited for me to grow up? I doubt that, I doubt it very much. Man is a strange thing, my girl. Man is like the lion in the desert or like the donkey: if no female's in sight, everything goes black. Gee, the donkey is ready to mount the first female crossing his way—so is the man with any random woman! The man's heart and soul have nothing to do with that other thing. Yorgos was dying of love in my arms but still took to bed Katerina, don't you remember, when that *thing* happened to me. Then he shared that he just squeezed his eyes tight and tried to see me as if he was making love to me. I sulked then, but now with Ovanes, I did the same!"

Briefly and without shame, as she would to a grown-up, Hrisoula told her those things. She was aware that Pinyo had picked up a lot anyway or she just thought that it was time to prepare her for the woman's life. When she was done, she sent Pinyo to bed, but Pinyo insisted,

"Then why did you get together with Ovanes?"

"Why? Just because! If only I knew what it was all

about, honest to God! His sadness is what I felt and his infinite loneliness, the cool, dank cave smell coming from him; only his soul was showing white in the dark. And it happened. Our souls got close together first, then our bodies wanted each other, and we felt good together. Only I still don't know if Ovanes also squeezed his eyes tight when he was caressing me!

"But what exactly is that thing in bed, huh, Hrisoula?"

"You'll find out on your own, it won't pass you by. In just a year or two, when you grow up. Just try to find your own only man or you'll squeeze your eyes tight throughout life and the sweet will taste bitter."

I remember twisting and turning in bed for a long time, going over Hrisoula's words. I slid a hand under the shirt and felt my small breasts like hard plums. They were just poking, hurting and itching but I swallowed the pain and rejoiced: I'll be a woman soon.

It looked like Hrisoula was preparing me for life, but she hadn't thought of everything.

Effy and Pinyo had become close and good friends. At that time he was fourteen, three years older than Pinyo. Since he had a bad stutter, he did not speak much, and when he was excited, he opened his eyes wide, his face turned pale and the brown freckles looked like ants crawling on his skin. He kept quiet, but Pinyo babbled nonstop; she had quite turned into Hrisoula. She was telling him about the doe, the Karakachans, about Syruie and her glass head, about Ovanes' telescope and mistress Elenitsa. As Effy listened, his pupils would widen or he'd grow very pale and sometimes beg, "Moole," when Pinyo deliberately stopped at the most interesting place and went on chattering idly about nothing at all.

In the early summer evenings, they watered the tomatoes and eggplants in the backyard garden together; Effy drew water from the well, Pinyo watered, the edge of her underskirt thrust behind her belt. At dusk one day, Effy was pouring water over her muddy feet straight from the copper pot when suddenly, a rusty brownish water stream was running down her ankles. "Effy, blood!" She raised her skirt higher; a thin stream of watery blood was winding down her thighs, "I'm dying, Effy!"

His face turned deadly white. He took her hand and his eyes tried to comfort her. Then he let her go and patting her hair with one hand, he tried to wipe the blood from her thighs with the other. He lay her down on the grass under the quince tree, but she was thrashing about, "Help, Effy, I'm dying! I might be dead already!" The boy ran to find Hrisoula. She came running and seeing Pinyo's eyes, wide with terror, she clapped her hands and burst out laughing, "What in the world!" She sent Effy away and quickly calmed her down: that was how girls turned into women. An orange was squeezed in their bodies and its juice drained out, once every month. She washed her and gave her clean rags to use. It came too early to her, but Pinyo had matured early.

I tried to avoid the little Albanian, but he did not understand why. Once he confronted me and with wide open eyes tried for quite a while to ask me how I felt.

"I'm good," I answered cautiously, but then let go and bragged, "I'm a woman now!"

One morning they heard the ring knocker on the gate. When they opened it, they saw the dry, sallow Irinyo, staring at them. They invited her to come in, but she abruptly tossed her head and hissed haughtily at Hrisoula,

"The master wants you to come for Syruie is too bad. Not that she is dying to see you or you can help her, but he wants you there. Take the girl with you, too, he said. When you left that day, master Ovanes went berserk and broke everything like a veritable elephant; that lamp was the first to go. Not that you are a real woman, white and sweet like mistress Elenitsa, but it's none of my business, so I keep my mouth shut. I don't say a word! Hurry up! Let's go!"

They ran. Their slippers anxiously stomped the cobbled street. Ovanes was waiting for them in the garden. Hrisoula passed by him and her skirt stirred up wind. They climbed the stairs to Syruie and gasped: all eyes, she was staring at them and swaying her swollen greenish head. She was a scary sight. She was old, so old, her face wrinkled, her gaze fixed, "She is ugly," Pinyo thought, "Gee, she's so ugly, poor Syruie!"

Then she heard her voice, a thin piece of thread,

"This is not me, Pinyo, don't be scared, I'm small and beautiful!"

Pinyo was scared.

Syruie ordered that they be left alone, the two of them. The guest sat on the bed and made an effort to touch her shriveled hand. "You've lost weight … a bit." Syruie did not respond. She thrust her hand under the pillow and took out a book with a colorful cover. Ovanes had ordered it from Paris; he was teaching her to read in French as he sometimes taught Pinyo, too. Now Pinyo opened it and found something between two of its pages. She took it carefully with two fingers and put it on her palm,

"Look, this is God."

A dry flower, almost turned into dust, was lying on her palm.

"Do you see how colorful it is by itself. It was not touched by a human hand; who has made it as it is? Look, in the middle a blue drop, then these pink veins and a yellow flame. If you watch carefully, you'll see red dots on the edge. And how small it is, the smallest I've ever found … who's created it if it was not man? God's manifestations are always before our eyes, but we treat them as something quite ordinary. Man stops wondering at the world and that is not good at all."

She placed her palm close to Pinyo's hand and the little flower stuck to the girl's pinkie. Syruie went on wheezing,

"Ovanes was right, nothing happens by chance in this world; there's a hidden meaning in everything. Nothing is by chance!"

"How about this flower?"

Pinyo heard Syruie laugh for the first time.

"But of course, little fool! It's not by chance either! God has created it so I find it, lock it between the pages of this book, show it to you one day and you understand that no chance things exist!"

"But … what's the purpose of my existence?"

"Don't you see?! The purpose of existence is in starting to ask what's the purpose of existence. One day the answer will find you."

She seemed delirious. Pinyo felt dizzy from her closeness and was afraid to move. They were sitting together, their shoulders touching—cold was blowing from Syruie's side, her body did not give off warmth anymore.

"Why is God like this Syruie? Why does he fill us with

fear? I never fear a good man, but I often fear God!"

Syruie smiled, "Your mistake is that you seek God with a man's image and you forget that it's the other way around. God is neither good nor bad. He is fair. The fear we feel of him is nothing else but our guilty conscience."

It was as if the air in the room had disappeared. Pinyo did not want to stay here anymore and Syruie sensed this. She put the flower away and touched the girl's hand.

"Forget everything I told you. You don't need it yet. Each of us will find our own God and he will be different, depending on each person's conscience. Nobody knows where he will find God. My father feels things right but can't express them well. He is too passionate, but he is not right when saying that God is at the center of the universe. If that is so, then the center is everywhere. Well, you just forget about all this!"

Syruie cast a last glance at Pinyo and the same primal cold streamed from her eyes again.

And Pinyo forgot and quite unexpectedly blurted out proudly,

"And I am a woman now!"

She was relieved to erase from her mind everything Syruie told her. She did not need it. It worried her. Syruie had found her God in a minute part of the world, in a little flower, because she was missing the whole. She was forced by the circumstances to find God in small things, to collect pieces of him. *My world was complete, roughly sewn: I had lived on the virgin mountain with its trees and thick bushes, the spider webs in the air and wild animals in the tree hollows, with the colorful snake necklaces on the rocks and all the sky at once. I had picked thousands of flowers but I hadn't looked into their core. Contrary to Syruie, I owned the whole and lacked the skill to go deep into the specific. I did not need God, at least for now.*

Then Syruie called Hrisoula. When Hrisoula came back, she grabbed the girl's hand and dragged her to the gate. Ovanes was there, watching them. Hrisoula slid by him never looking up. Pinyo did the same. On the street, Hrisoula sighed with relief and stopped, thoughtful. "This girl, Syruie, asked me to go back to her father."

The very same day at dusk, Irinyo rushed in again. "Hurry up, quick!" They ran and Pinyo's heart was throbbing in her throat. When they rushed into the yard, they stopped in their tracks.

Syruie is sitting in her wicker bamboo chair like a figurine with a big swollen head, the rays of the sunset pierce her body and all of her shines. She has really become transparent as if she was not made of flesh and blood, as if Ovanes the glazier had blown her from the clearest glass. Ovanes himself is sitting behind her chair and holding her head, wobbling faintly on her thin, sorry neck.

Syruie saw them and smiled, her voice dragging like a silk thread,

"Despinyooo …, how nice you've become … a woman!"

And her voice broke. Her body suddenly collapsed, her crystal head hit the cobbled yard with a ring and white water drained out, pure and sparkling—a thin stream headed for the nearby dwarf-like pomegranate tree they had planted last year. The water sank quickly into the soil and as they were watching, the tree straightened up and grew a whole span.

Pinyo told Effy how beautiful Syruie was. When the water ran out and sank into the soil around the dwarf pomegranate, her head became small and delicate like a doll's, her face thin, the arcs of her eyebrows spread like wings, her lips turned pink and her skin lucid, like porcelain. Only in death was she a real girl, as if she had thrown her ashen mask away—stunned, Irinyo crossed herself, *a veritable mistress Elenitsa!*

Pinyo was talking as her hands were automatically carding the wool. They were sitting in the narrow room together and Effy was helping her to finish, so they could play tipcat in the backyard.

"Syruie and mistress Elenitsa must have already hugged each other, right, Effy? It's been forty days now."

Effy stuttered. He wanted to say something but just waved a hand.

The girl stared curiously at his face. The freckles made him look quite like a child. What if I ask him to kiss me? I can learn about that thing between a man and a woman. Right now! She dropped the fluffy wool in her lap and called the little Albanian with her forefinger, "Come here for a second!" She pulled him to sit next to her and looked straight into his eyes,

"Kiss me, Effy!"

He hesitantly kissed her cheek.

"On the mouth!"

She wrapped her hands around his neck and their lips met. His were soft and warm and she was a little queasy when she felt them as a piece of living flesh. She drew back. "This is what adults do," she explained and they went on carding the wool.

The next day, Esad came in. His smile was wry, his

eyes squinted. He joined her on the floor, sat right on top the carded wool and put his palm on her hand right away, "Effy told me how you play!" Pinyo was confused, but perked up quickly, "It's just pretend, you know." Esad took her other hand, too.

"I'll show you how it is for real, how about that?"

She moved back straining to hear Effy and the others but heard no sound. She wanted to jump up and run, but Esad threw her down on the pile of wool. His hard lips sucked hers, his mustache poked her. The prentice swung his leg over her thigh and she felt that hard, tight thing. She got really scared, pulled away and screamed. Esad put his hand lightly on her mouth and slid his other hand in her bosom; her breasts were small like sour pears but Esad got impatient and started pawing her hard. She bit him, he pulled out his hand, and she screamed as if she was being murdered. The Albanian came to his senses and jumped up,

"Shut up, you, cry baby! I know what I'm doing! Nothing bad would happen to you; we were just going to play a little!"

He left her in the wool and walked out. Only then she cringed. She had inhaled his heavy, strong male scent: his body had strained its muscles like a young animal listening to nature; he could have mounted and penetrated her if she had relaxed.

She stood up, fixed her skirt, went to the window and stared outside but saw nothing. If Hrisoula had heard, Pinyo would get a sound thrashing. She was looking for trouble and if she went on like this, she could find it by all means; this was perfectly clear to her now.

Soon they moved to Ovanes's home again. Hrisoula

had promised that to Syruie and was bent on keeping her word. The Armenian met them with silence, but Irinyo even rejoiced—her heart felt heavy in the deserted house. They settled in the room they had before, but soon Hrisoula started to spend her nights in Ovanes' room. He perked up a little, his eyes cleared up and he got down to work. With Syruie's French books, he renewed his lessons with Pinyo and because she picked up fast, he praised her all the time. Gradually life in the house got into the old rhythm. The girls shook the carpets, dusted, washed, watered the flowers in the garden. Pinyo took special care of the pomegranate tree: she pulled the weeds around its root, caressed its leaves, talked to it and noted with surprise that none of its leaves turned yellow. Fall leaves covered everything around, only the tree was green and fluttered its silvery leaves.

One day somebody knocked, anxiously hitting the gate with the ring knocker for a while. Ovanes opened and let into the yard a small man with stooping shoulders and nose like a beak. He was Kevork, the jeweler, a friend of the master. They sat at the heavy table in the parlor, Hrisoula made coffee, Pinyo brought the cups and as she was serving them, she heard the jeweler's low voice,

"Big crowds surge in, like a river! They put them in Muslim homes, with relatives, or in the barracks. They are fleeing Lozengrad; the war is a matter of a few days, you know!"

On the next day as Pinyo was walking down to the river to catch fish with the copper bowl, she saw the very same crowds Kevork was talking about. Whole Turkish families were sitting on their luggage piled on ox-driven carts, the wives' eyes anxiously sparkled through the slits in the niqabs, the kids were unusually quiet and walked by the carts with the men.

Throughout the day the carts were dragging one after another along the bridge into the town and were easily seen from the Christian neighborhood. Edirne was packed with refugees.

Pinyo ran to Esad and Effy and learned that a big, terrible war was under way. Esad was rubbing his palms contentedly, "Now they'll see; I'm also leaving, joining one of the armies, the Greek one perhaps or the Bulgarian or Serbian, for now the allies determine Albania's fate. I am Albanian, right? No way I'd sit in master Vassilaki's shop doing clip clip with the scissors; I'd rather do it on the battleground, yeah! Clip-clip, five with a stroke of the knife!"

Esad got excited and started clipping the air with the scissors, his eyes bulging. Frightened, they were trying to calm him down and indeed, he disappeared the next day, leaving Effy alone in the shop.

At home, Ovanes ordered the basic necessities packed. "If the front line reaches Edirne, we'll have to move to Chorlu; cousin Dirkhan lives there; he'll house us for a while. It's best to wait for now."

The war broke in the beginning of October. The Bulgarian army, on its way to liberate their compatriots in East Thrace, took Lozengrad in two days. The Turks pricked up their ears, the Christians secretly rejoiced. Ovanes started nailing boards on the windows, "Edirne is next, we were not able to withdraw on time." The Turkish army was moving out of Lozengrad and heading our way, to reinforce Edirne fortress. Now nobody could leave or enter the town. Ovanes had tried to bribe the guards, but none was tempted.

In the middle of October, a muffled rumble shook the neighborhood. Howitzers fired and the wind blew the smell of gunpowder all the way to the town. Then a heavy gray bird hovered in the sky above their heads.

"Airplane, airplane!" the local kids shouted enthusiastically.

Pinyo wanted to run with them but Hrisoula pulled her back by the ear. They had seen an airplane at the spring fair, circling in the sky like an ugly duckling and dropping white and red garlands. "Let me see the garlands," Pinyo insisted this time, but Hrisoula pushed her in the back with one knee and Pinyo landed in the yard.

They climbed up to the verandah and from there saw how the gray flying machine wobbled back to the fortress and suddenly dumped a hail of fire on it. Ovanes grabbed his head, "Madmen! Fire from the sky I've never heard of! Those will win this war, I bet!

"Who are they, Ovanes?"

"The Bulgarians, they say. Whoever they are, they are all Christians and theirs is a liberating war for freedom. God will lead them in battle!"

"But Ovanes, wasn't God against people killing each other? This is what you said!"

"Let's not let God intervene in our human affairs, Despinyo! You are right but first and foremost, God does not allow anybody to deprive another of freedom. I don't think he'd scold the Christians, for just is their war. Pure freedom is what they fight for."

From the verandah, Pinyo noticed how the little green pomegranate tree shook all its leaves,

"Pure freedom does not exist, Ovanes!"

She even startled herself.

Ovanes and Hrisoula looked at her quizzically.

"Why do you talk like that? Ovanes asked tensely. If it's freedom you are deprived of, you are allowed to use all possible means to get it back."

"But the words you choose are not precise, Ovanes! Freedom can't be pure! The corpses rolling on the battlefields now, the glazed eyes of those humans rotting in their own innards, they are freedom. Don't be so passionate and talk about freedom as you talk about a child. Do you understand?"

"No!"

"But it's so simple! Freedom is outside and inside, Ovanes! Through the flower's stamen, you know! You look through the stamen, then walk through it and you are free!"

Pinyo's talk was getting even more incomprehensible and she was getting even more scared of her words.

Hrisoula spoke, "That's what I also said, right Pinyo?"

Hers was an untimely intervention interrupting the girl's flow of thought. Quickly, like a raspy chatterbox, she babbled the rest; she couldn't hold her tongue: God was cruel, he gave men the yearning for freedom, this insatiable yearning, but they took it for freedom; the truth is rather—yearning did not breed freedom, but freedom bred yearning; freedom inside a man bred yearning for freedom outside. Only free people could fight for their freedom.

"You taunt and challenge me!" The Armenian almost cried, "You are playing with words!"

Then he came to himself and asked humbly,

"Why is this Bulgarian freedom not pure?"

"Because they are not the only ones responsible for it. The conquerors of freedom are part of it. The only reason we know freedom is because unfreedom has always existed somewhere, sometime, just like here and now," Pinyo barely had time to answer with a voice that was not hers.

Ovanes tried to offer truce,

"What is happening right now with all people is important, no matter what you call it!"

Then, rolling her eyes, Pinyo made a last effort to say,

"What happens to all people is not important, Ovanes, but what happens to each man is!"

She ran to Hrisoula and cuddled in her apron.

The little pomegranate tree stopped fluttering and its leaves relaxed.

It was quiet around Edirne now. A thick web of wire nets divided the rival armies. Behind their forts, the Turks were probably blessing the German ingenuity which had built them. The Bulgarians had closed the ring around the forts and lay in wait. The townsfolk relaxed a little. Those who had remained in the town swept through the streets, the shops put their goods out in the shop windows, the bazaar was open again. Despinyo was swaying her skirts in the neighborhood, and overcoming her fear, reached as far as the center sometimes. She was nosing around, catching the body scents, people's worries and fears, their melancholy and anxious anticipation. Quite unexpectedly, her nostrils sniffed that mysterious whiff of salty air, which mixed with other scents, and only her extremely sensitive sense of smell could catch. She guessed that it was nothing else but that love.

She understood that something else, extraordinary, was happening to her.

One morning when she heard the monotonous sounds of the morning prayer from the minaret of Sultan Selim Mosque, angry ants crawled up and down her flesh and she plugged her fingers in her ears. She was used to the life in the Orient, and she never thought of the part of the earth fate had thrown her into, nor was this of any importance to her. But suddenly, without any reason, things changed. The long-drawn wails of the Hodja sent towards the sky seemed mysterious to her, dark and sticky. As if it was not a man up there in the minaret, but only a voice, ancient and sobbing, weeping to God about despair, about the dark, human grief. It was depressing and scary, and Pinyo sensed for the first time how alien it was to her. If at this very moment she could see the man's face, she surely would not feel like that, but she saw just his voice, his disconsolate, human soul. And she felt for all men on this earth.

Unchildish sadness overwhelmed her. She stopped talking, her lips were glued together. She sat in the remotest corner of the room with a glazed look in her eyes, staring into a single spot. The moment that howling started, she pressed her palms to her ears and felt she was going mad. "Tell him to stop, I can't stand it anymore!" And indeed, one day she broke down and started pummeling her head with her fists.

Ovanes sat by her,

"Is it the war you are afraid of, Pinyo?"

"It is as if all people weep in it, Ovanes, in this voice from the minaret! It scares me; he is a Turk."

Ovanes was silent for a while trying to grasp what she

meant.

"This voice is raised towards the sky, Despinyo! Don't be afraid of it, no matter how alien it sounds because it comes from the earth's core but soars up."

The girl buried her face in his lap, something neither expected. He put his hand on her head and his voice shook,

"That's what man is, Pinyo! Kneaded from dark soil and white water."

"But what if he prays to God that his people win? What will happen to the others, then?"

"I told you, this voice soars up to the sky. And somebody up there knows how to judge what's fair."

"All Turks scare me now!"

"Well, we are all human, Pinyo; we just speak different languages but do not differ so much … Don't fear people because they are Turks, Greeks, or Armenian, but fear them when they want to harm you. Then seek protection …"

Although Ovanes did not say anything very important, she felt relieved. She had shared her fear and thus reduced it in half. She perked up again, just like that. Hrisoula sighed with relief and flicked Pinyo's nose with her fingers, "I was getting scared you'd start drilling your brains with a corkscrew, you know!"

Pinyo started hanging out in the neighborhood again and one day, quite unawares, reached the main street and stopped at old Ali's pastry shop. He had the most scrumptious baklava in Edirne. When he saw her staring longingly at the shop window, old Ali stepped out beaming, "If you could eat the pastry just by looking, my shop window would be empty now !" He slipped a packet of pastry in her hands, stroked her hair and after winking at her, went back in.

Irinyo brought the news that the Turkish army, retreating from Lozengrad was already here, behind the Bulgarians. "After the help they got, the Turks in the fort braced up, so what will be, will be. They will trap those Bulgarians; all their courage and bravado are wasted, along with their freedom ! They say that all the Turks around count sixty thousand and we are in the same pot, mother of God!"

Irinyo was quite scared; she often crossed herself, slammed the pots and pans around and muttered her peppery curses. Hrisoula was anxious, too. Ovanes did not seem changed; Pinyo and he were still tackling the French language, and the girl could already read and write with ease. Something else hovered inside the house, though; it had nothing to do with the war and Pinyo was catching wind of it with her new sense of smell.

The fighting lasted four days. It was fierce: the earth shook underfoot, not a living soul walked the streets. In the evening the more self-possessed watched the war from their verandahs. It was an incredible spectacle. The roar of the cannons went on non-stop for hours, the glow of the searchlights set the sky ablaze like a massive fire, the exploding projectiles looked like fireworks from afar. Then suddenly silence fell. For a while, they strained their ears to hear but not a shot broke the silence. Finally they learned the exciting news that the Turks had withdrawn and the Bulgarians were still holding the fort under siege.

As if coming out of a big anthill, the people started moving around the town. They picked up their old jobs, a little scared but not panicked. They had lived together for a long time: Bulgarians, Turks, Greeks, Armenians—years, centuries. They had communicated in a composed manner, accommodating and peaceful, but something invisible had divided them—it was something so deeply intimate that they had never talked openly about it, nor had any serious fights about it.

Somehow, they had managed to achieve balance in their relationship, these different religious societies, and the Muslims had communicated with their townsmen of other religions in a reserved but neighborly respectful manner. The religious feeling turned out to be cherished and intimate, just like love, and just like it, it could be shared with the one and only ... none other than God.

Somehow though, things changed. Nobody from the Christian neighborhood made any attempt to cross the invisible line separating them from the Turkish quarter, nor did the Turks greet the Christian tradesfolk, who were opening neighboring stores. Each of them felt strange. Somebody else had always determined the fate of the little people: to attack each other or to make peace. Once again, they were forced to fight each other as before, as always when someone invisible decides the fate of the little people with the indifference and arrogance of the all-powerful, with the confidence of God's proxy. Sometimes, through their scared minds like lightning passed the blasphemous thought that, you see, God is supposed to decide, but, there ... and they crossed themselves, or their foreheads hit the ground and they prayed that the bloody river dragging its body through the Thracian fields would pass by them. Let everything happen, if possible, in a humane way, without blood, if possible ...

"If it could happen that way, it should have happened

by now," Irinyo voiced her thoughts one day and they were shocked to hear this from her mouth.

One day a few Bulgarian boys came running. They had been playing on the shore and some Turkish boys had started shooting stones at them. The boys held their cracked heads and wiped their faces, smearing blood and tears. "Damn the bloodsuckers," jumped the fathers. "It's just children playing," screamed the mothers, barely able to restrain them.

The men pretended to calm down but gathered together, exchanged a few words and disappeared. They went straight to the Turkish neighborhood and sat together with the attackers' fathers to drink coffee and talk about this business in a roundabout way. Thus, gradually, they revealed their purpose.

"Is your life bad here? Nobody dares lay a finger on you! What bothers you, neighbor, so you had to go to war?" One of the Turks uttered gravely and slurped his coffee. His eyes revealed an amiable man.

"So much blood will be spilled that it'll fill up the Maritza, Arda and Tundzha, instead of water!" another added gloomily and also slurped.

The Bulgarians kept silent. Then one of them coughed and uttered faintly,

"The time for it had come, Efendi!"

The others gasped.

"Do you hear what you are saying?! Go ahead, say, what do you lack here?"

"Motherland is what we lack, Efendi!"

The Bulgarian barely whispered these words. He was an assistant hakim with the French doctor; his name was Cyril, a well-educated but rather quiet man. Now he suddenly spoke in a way he never suspected he could. He was trying to stop himself but the words were getting out of his mouth as if despite his will. At last, these words came to be spoken by a giaur—they were strong words, they had been gathering strength for 500 years. The Turk turned crimson like his fez and banged the table with his knuckles, "Shut up, big head! You have everything you need! Including freedom! Has anybody in this town ever laid a finger on you, so you want to shed blood for freedom! Pure, pristine freedom is what you have here!"

Then Cyril spoke gently,

"Freedom is not a virgin, neighbor. Freedom is deflowered while still in the cradle. We rape her, we spread her legs as if she were a dirty slut, forgive me; we violate her. We take turns on her like she was a real slut because we think she is only ours. If we realize that she belongs to nobody, then perhaps she'd belong to all of us. Freedom is infinite, there's enough of it for all of us! But we, here, we've reached for her since the world began, like dirty womanizers. We've reached for her and destroyed the most sacred thing God has given us, and then we pray that the Almighty be with us because you see, allegedly, we fight for Him. Both parties. He can't do that, huh, Efendi? The Almighty has nothing to do with this; it's all our, human work. We are vile people, Turk, since we so violently steal each other's freedom. That about the slut is not quite true, though. We might have stolen somebody's wife, or even somebody's mother."

He was silent for a while and then added even more quietly,

"To make things crystal clear, you stole it from us, Efendi. You stole our white-haired mother and you violated her. This is the truth and you can't deny it …"

They came back wiping the blood from their faces, just like their sons before. The women screamed, and wailed, and scolded their men, "Worse than kids, you all are!"

Ovanes forbade Pinyo to leave the house and in order to keep her at home, started her on the French reading and writing, but much more difficult now. The Armenian was happy she was picking up so fast, "Even Syruie could not catch the pronunciation so well!"

"Bon zhur, madam Irinyo, bon zhur madmoazel Hrisoula, bon zhur, mosyu Ovanes," I was greeting left and right. One day, I approached the little pomegranate tree and whispered,

"Bon zhur Syruie!"

The wind was twisting the tree tops. It was the end of October, a long and rather restless fall was coming. One morning, they were sitting quietly in the room downstairs. Hrisoula had propped one elbow against her knee, her head resting in her hand. Her beauty was somehow subdued now; it had become softer and brighter. She braided her hair in two thick braids, which she put up on the back of her head with hairpins and only thin strands of curly locks hung down at her temples.

At one point, she lifted her head, wonder in her eyes,

"It's been such a long time, huh, Pinyo!"

What she had in mind was not clear.

"What did we have to go through, huh, Pinyo? And Ovanes is teaching you French now! He is a good man, educated, raised in France, not like us, in the wilderness! I care for him, my girl, I'll give my soul for him if I have to!"

Her eyes were sad.

"We were not able to go away, my girl, neither to Venice, nor to Galilenogalilen or Chorlu. Your Bulgarians are fighting near Chorlu right now, mauling the Turks. I pity the Turks, you know! I pity all losers! Well, those men keep fighting, but we sit here and don't dare budge because Edirne is still under siege with no end in sight. Whoever managed to leave, they left and that's that! Now the town is so heavily guarded that even birds don't fly over it! What a pity we couldn't leave, Despinyo! If we leave, we could find what we look for!"

"We don't look for anything! Haven't you forgotten Yorgos, yet?"

"Not yet, my girl. I don't know why, but he's always on my mind these days!"

"Not that you don't show it!"

"I can't wait to see him!"

"You'll see him in your dreams!"

Hrisoula turned to the wall.

Then Irinyo knocked and said that the master ordered them to talk to a cheesemonger and buy as much cheese as they thought they needed. "You are the mistress now," and she swung her skirts and left. Both girls slid into their slippers and flopped through the yard to the gate.

There stood Yorgos.

Hrisoula turned deadly pale. Yorgos stared at her and his jaws twitched under his beard. Pinyo recovered first, "Come in, Yorgos, come in, man!"

He stood still as a statue. Finally, Hrisoula's lips parted,

"What brought you here?"

He had entered the town back in October, before the siege, and had to stay: the guards had not let him go back. With other Karakachans, he had brought raw hides and cheese down to the valley, but they had got stuck in Edirne because of the war, so after the girls had moved out, Yorgos had come to stay with master Vassilaki and help Effy in the shop.

Hrisoula got over the shock,

"Show us your cheese!"

Pinyo looked at her in amazement. It was as if she'd never longed for this man, not even a minute ago. Cold and serious, Hrisoula ordered, "Give us two tins of brined feta cheese and a round of yellow cheese. You'll settle up with the master later."

Her face was blank, her lips pressed unpleasantly tight. Yorgos cast a brief glance at Pinyo but she looked away. He turned around and left. They followed him to the street. Yorgos unloaded the tins and the yellow cheese, took them to the yard, came back and silently led the mule out. Only then did Pinyo call out,

"Yorgos, the master hasn't paid you!"

He did not look back.

It was spring when the Karakachan appeared on their street again. "Tell Hrisoula that I'll wait for her tonight under master Vassilaki's orchard; tell her to be careful because soldiers scurry along the shore; tomorrow the fighting will start again!"

Hrisoula listened to Pinyo intently. Her eyes shone for a moment, then she shut her lips tight, "No way will I go! I don't want him anymore!"

She went to Irinyo and left the girl utterly confused. She came back shortly, put on new slippers, spat on her fingers to straighten her eyebrows and smoothed her skirt with a trembling hand, "I'm going to the neighbor's."

She returned when everybody was eating silently

at the solid table. Ovanes asked nothing, Hrisoula said nothing. Pinyo was trying to guess what had happened from her face, but it was cold and expressionless.

They helped Irinyo wash the dishes and sneaked into the small room. Hrisoula stood by the window, staring into the night. The gray March drizzle spilled upon the windows real baby snakes with twisting tails. Only now did Hrisoula remember that her hair was wet; she wrapped it around her wrist and squeezed it dry.

"I did not tell him anything. I'm a weak person, Pinyo."

Later they joined Ovanes at the furnace. They helped him to sieve the sand left from the fall. When the sacks were full, the Armenian put them up against the wall and brushed the sand off his hands. All at once, he looked Hrisoula in the eyes and went on looking until she bent her head.

"Go inside, it's too cold for you." Ovanes said quietly and turned his back on them, "I'll manage on my own. I said, on my own!"

That night Hrisoula stayed with Pinyo. Ovanes did not come to look for her. The girls did not sleep a wink till the morning because Hrisoula was feverish. Pinyo piled blankets on her and massaged her heels with the grappa she found in the kitchen. As she was massaging her temples, Pinyo felt like crying out loud, but instead only scolded her meekly, "What's wrong with you, don't be a baby!"

Just before the morning when the dawn was seeping through the windows, Hrisoula squeezed her hand.

"Tell me Pinyo, whatever you say, that's what I'll do!"

I gasped in fear. So hesitant I saw her for the first time. She was even sick from not being able to decide. That night, I, Pinyo, grew up irreparably. I recalled the words of the peasant woman who knew how to talk with all nature, "We are all specks of dust that don't know their real dimensions, the dimensions of love and suffering."

Hrisoula continued,

"Yorgos is lonely, Ovanes is lonely, and I am lonely. Perhaps love is sometimes called loneliness. You see how complex everything is? I want to be with him, but I can't!"

Pinyo snapped,

With who! Ovanes or Yorgos?

Startled, Hrisoula sighed,

"I don't know, I really don't, Despinyo!"

The girl tried to remind Hrisoula how she'd said that Yorgos was her only half and that she squeezed her eyes tight when with Ovanes, but Hrisoula interrupted her,

"But, maybe, that's not the most important, Pinyo? Find me a way out, can you, because my heart is with Yorgos, but my soul with Ovanes! Can you, Pinyo, tell me!"

Now, this was too much for Pinyo. Hrisoula wanted too much from her; she wanted her to sort out her life, that's what she wanted. In pain, confused and on the verge of hysterics, Hrisoula just pummeled Pinyo's chest with her fists, "Tell me now, quick, spit it out!"

The girl slapped her, gave her some water to drink and thrust another pillow under her head. Hrisoula lowered her eyelids and as she was falling asleep, she managed to say,

"We made love, Yorgos and I tonight in the sand, Pinyo! There, in the sand, we made love! And as we were doing it, I squeezed my eyes tight and saw Ovanes!"

On the same day, around Edirne, the war came to

the boiling point. After the long lull, during which the people had almost forgotten the trap they were caught in, the Bulgarians suddenly attacked the fort. The earth shook, thick clouds of smoke hid the sky, the smell of gunpowder lay on the roofs like a heavy wing. Everybody hid, the town was deserted. Word had it that seventy thousand Turkish soldiers defended the forts, but nobody had any idea how many Bulgarians there were. The heavy cannons in all five hundred forts were spewing fire like dragons against the Bulgarian army. It was unseen and unheard of, it was pure hell. The women, worried out of their minds, were scurrying frantically around the house. In vain did Ovanes try to calm them down; in the roar of the cannons, they did not hear his voice. Irinyo fainted and when she came to, she hid in the big caldron they used to make soap and put the lid on. Despite fear, Hrisoula and Pinyo looked at each other in dismay and burst out laughing; their laughter grew braver, they doubled over and tears sprang from their eyes. The laughter calmed them. They put plugs in their ears and sat with Ovanes in the salon. He smiled at them and raised a sheet of paper to their eyes: he'd written on it in French that they should not be worried since neither the Bulgarians nor the Turks would bother the mixed blood.

Just before noon, the roar suddenly stopped and the silence deafened their ears. The silence lasted long and they did not know what to think. At noon, Effy came running. He was so agitated that they could understand nothing from his stutter. Master Vassilaki rushed in after him.

"Shukri Pasha surrendered! He gave his sword to the Bulgarian truce-bearers! The fortress fell, the Bulgarians are in town!"

They ran out. In the Christian neighborhood, the people were on the streets, shouting like mad and running towards the center. The Bulgarian flag was waving on top of Sultan Selim Mosque.

At this very moment something strange happened to Pinyo. She swirled like a top, raised her hand, pointed at the flag fluttering in the sharp wind and yelled,

"Our flag! This is our flag! My flag! I am Bulgarian!"

This patriotic outburst was quite unexpected for her. Up until this moment she'd never thought about her ancestry. She'd lived long in the mountains and now lived in Edirne with the Karakachan Hrisoula, the Armenian Ovanes and the Greek Irinyo; her friend was the little Albanian Effy and the fact that they were different did not stop them from feeling close. But now the storm of the war had moved the whole human mass and driven by its wind, Pinyo felt lighter, like a feather shed by a sparrow. Ecstasy lifted her and made her separate and independent from her nears and dears; it lifted her above the sharp minarets of Sultan Selim Mosque, above the three rivers, the Arda, Tundzha and Maritsa, above the town of Edirne, above the whole excited crowd, which cried, laughed, yelled and whispered one word only, freedom. So strong was the united human energy at this moment that she physically felt its power. Her head swam, her legs softened and she slumped down the wall of a store. They would have run over her just like that, but a man stumbled at her, lifted her heavy body and seeing only the whites of her eyes, slapped her so hard that sparks came out of her eyes. "Run straight home, you little brat, and jump and yell there as hard as you want!" She turned around and left without seeing a single Bulgarian soldier, although she'd run to the street to see them, to be able to recognize them. Now, though, that was of no importance.

Dragging back home, I was thinking of the new feeling in me. I realized that until now I had owned something too big, mother nature itself, and I did not miss a motherland because I had the whole world instead. From now on I wouldn't be able to accept not having a motherland or having it just as a newly awakened feeling. I knew that in life everybody belongs somewhere: I had learned from Hrisoula that the man belonged to the woman and the woman to the man and that in nature, it was even easier and simpler: the water belonged to the sea, the sweet briar to the woods, the eagle to the sky. Today, in a daze, I realized that the motherland belongs to the people who are its children and belong to her. I was too young to understand that having found my national identity, I had lost the bigger and infinite, the unconscious cosmopolitanism that had created me as a human being. The world was shrinking, getting smaller and soon I would be facing the impossibility to be satisfied with only the small and intimate or with my old world without beginning or end. I'd want to have them both, but I did not know how impossible that was.

For the second time in her life Pinyo experienced a miracle, quite suddenly, as it happens with miracles. It was the very same day when Hrisoula made her final choice. What made it the ultimate miracle in the girl's fate was the fact that the war was declared over on that very day.

The day of the triple miracle was serene, a blue and green day in April and like every day, a miracle in itself. The peaches and apricots were blooming wildly in the neighborhood and ever since the morning, the people felt happy, without knowing why. This joy without reason was in fact the premonition that could never be misled by appearances. Voices were ringing, the women were engaged in intimate conversations about nothing and everything and through the fences, the men shook their heads and recalled how a month ago Shukri Pasha surrendered his sword to the Bulgarian truce bearers. Somewhat nonchalantly, they worried that the recent rains could cause the rivers to overflow and flood the orchards in the low neighborhoods; they exchanged small gossip; a man in a faraway yard sang with a trembling voice. This agitation was quite unusual because such bright days were not new in April. All who had left the town before the siege had come back and the neighborhood looked like a teeming hive; it was as if people were trying to kill time while waiting for something hugely important. And it came.

First the wings of a slight green breeze brought the news that the war had ended, once and forever, and that the allied Christian forces had won. Excitement erupted like sparkling champagne; one after another, people were shouting hooray, putting the emphasis on the r like soldiers; they were hugging each other, jumping around like children and doing other childish things; Ovanes poured sparkling wine, as he had promised, the same he'd gotten from Marseilles with the blueprints for the telescope. Dazed by the common joy, Pinyo was shouting in French," Viv la victoar!"

The day was getting bluer and sparkled brighter.

Only Hrisoula walked around dejected, watching Ovanes with big sad eyes, wondering how to tell him about what she had finally decided. At last she threw herself at his feet,

"Forgive me, Ovanes!"

This happened in the middle of the yard and everybody saw: Pinyo and Irinyo, and the little pomegranate tree, fluttering its fine leaves. Ovanes stopped as if he'd suddenly grown roots. Hrisoula rushed to pack her things. After a while, she called Pinyo and started defending herself boldly,

"Ovanes is good. I am the bad one! So I'm going with Yorgos!"

Irinyo was in the kitchen and we could hear her slamming the pot tops around. Hrisoula started scolding Pinyo,

"I'm not to blame! Is that clear! Don't even say a word!"

The girl, though, was as silent as a fish.

Hrisoula ran to Ovanes again,

"Forgive me, Ovanes!"

The man turned around and entered the house. Hrisoula waited for a while and then approached the little pomegranate tree,

"That's how it should be! Ovanes will find his half; I just humiliate him in front of other people. I'm not his match, really! See, our souls match, no mistake about it! Our souls seek to hug each other, but they do that from a secret place, so nobody would believe this! Who would respect a love like this, so deep that on the surface it does not look like itself. People will take it for something else! They already gossip about Ovanes for my sake and he does not deserve this!"

The little pomegranate tree did not stir at all despite the light breeze

Hrisoula ran to the cook,

"I'm leaving with Yorgos. God had made us in the same mold, he is just like me! And then, each of us carries the same guilt, but separately. Just think about it: we've doubled it since we live away from each other. I'm leaving with Yorgos, Irinyo, so we unite the guilt of not getting to know each other on time and hurting so many good people. Oh my!

Irinyo said nothing but at least stopped slamming the pans. Hrisoula, exhausted from all that talk, went to her room and lay in bed on her belly. Pinyo came in and threw heavy words in her face,

"So you forgot about me, huh?"

Hrisoula gasped and sprang to her feet,

"I gave it a lot of thought, Pinyo! We both thought, Yorgos and I! You are smart and quick, see how fast you learned to talk in French; Ovanes will send you to Marseilles to study, or maybe, Venice! Just think! You can't go back anymore, you'll grow wild with us, and we're not going back to our mountain. We'll join other Karakachans."

Pinyo burst out crying and so did Hrisoula, at last.

At that time, the festivities continued outside. The streets were full of people, the sky was shining even brighter and Pinyo felt a bit relieved. Ovanes was not a bad man; he loved her like his own child ...

She went on walking without suspecting that at this very moment, fate was counting the last seconds of her old life and getting ready to create, just to please herself a little, a miracle—fate is quite stingy in that respect and seldom engages in anything like this.

When she reached the main street, Pinyo winked at old Ali and stopped to hear the lively discussion of a big group of people. They were talking in Bulgarian. On the square behind them, oxcarts stood unharnessed and women sat in them, bright red aprons strapped around their waists.

I felt a sudden shortness of breath. It wheezed out of my mouth the moment I heard the words these strangers exchanged.

Two women wearing the same red aprons stood at a fence, a little away from this group. One of them stretched and caught a handful of the blooming rose bush jutting through the fence and buried her nose in its velvet core, "Mmm, such a sweet smell!" The other, tall and thin, her eyes very bright on a weather-beaten face was searching rather uneasily in the rose bush. Gold beetles swarmed in it, changing their color to bright blue.

"Look, blue beetles!" the same woman muttered very quietly. I heard her and strained all over. "Look, a blue one, haven't seen one for a while!"

I headed straight towards the woman. I sensed her body scent; her clothes smelled of geranium soap, but that fragrance could not suppress the other thing: I remembered that the same scent of bread, milk and love I once inhaled from the bosom of the very same woman.

At that moment all the words from my mother's tongue surged up my throat: blue beetle, milk, bread, hollyhock, water, sky, Elada, mother, forgive me, farewell, I can't!

I spoke them in a daze.

The woman slapped her hands together,

"Goodness Gracious!"

And she slumped down the fence to the ground.

~ PART TWO ~

THE LETTER

I got your letter an hour ago, and I already know it by heart, and I'm writing in reply to your dear letter. I hold it in my hands and it is so extraordinary that this letter has traveled through the whole of Europe and reached its destination without getting lost on a plane, night train, or even here, at the post office in Burgas, they could have misplaced it and forgotten about it, but it found me and I'm holding it and it is even more extraordinary that you, nobody else, wrote those lines in lavender ink, and it's as if you were at home, not only on this sheet of paper, son.

Son,

Many years have passed since you went away with that Regina Spain; with time, you've grown up and become a man. You are handsome in the photo but I can't believe it's you. When the sons grow up away from their mothers, they mature faster, and it's happened to you. I know that you are more mature for your age; you even scared me with your questions but mostly with your thoughts, which I could not hear, of course, but saw them touching your forehead like shadows of clouds. I have you in my memory like you were before Regina Spain; you are sixteen there, and I don't know how I'd feel when we meet; you write you're coming with Miriam in the spring and I can't wait to welcome you back. It looks like the wars here are over; the fires stopped smoking and I hope you could travel safely.

I was very happy that you'd mastered the language of gestures and finished a school of pantomime; I don't know exactly what it is; you write that it's artistic movements for the stage which speak to an audience; so, you speak two languages now and with the language of silence you chose, they add up to three. I'm thinking of studying your language although my faith is strong that one day you will get over all this and start speaking again. No bodily reason should be in your way. Speak with your hands until then if that's what you prefer, but don't forget your words, son; the most human thing is to use words to express yourself. I intend to learn this new language of yours; there's a family of refugees here from Edirne, their boy is deaf-and-dumb and often speaks with his hands; he'll teach me—not that you won't understand me as I am, but I want to share your silence. Our neighborhood is crowded now; the refugees from Edirne were settled here, and low uniform houses were built for them on the lakeshore; Sharon, the rich Jew from France, gave the money so the people could find shelter here, and we live well together now, and life is more interesting.

Writing about the refugees reminds me that the blue girl is here, do you remember when she bumped into you on the square, laughed and said pardone moa! The very same girl I am talking about, I can't forget her somehow, Elada her name is, what a name; see, when she was born they called a relative, a Greek woman, to baptize her and she came up with that name so that the girl would grow up wise and famous, but the girl wants to be called Pinyo because the Karakachans, who found her abandoned by the first refugees in 1903, called her Despina or Despinyo. She speaks French because some educated Armenian from Edirne taught her to write and speak in that language. She knows it surprisingly well.

They became friends, Ferso and she; they are young ladies now and very beautiful next to each other: Ferso, like a willow, with her fiery hair and green eyes and that olive-skinned Elada

Pinyo with her azure eyes; just so you know, Ferso often asks about you. "Write to him that I'm waiting for him," that's what she says every time we meet and her dimples laugh. The pastry cook, Manyo, moved her shop to the center and Ferso goes there to help her since she wants to be a pastry cook; I think it will suit her well because whose hands knead the dough is important—its taste does not depend only on the flour, sugar and yeast, but also on the person who kneads it.

All depends on the person, son. Love, too. They say love is one for all people but each uses it differently. I'll talk to you about love now, not only because I thought of Ferso, but because I want to talk to you about your father and me. What you saw then, that's not all that happens between a man and a woman. I want you to know that we married for love. Although I am a Jew, nobody could stop Tano from taking me as his wife. But his way of using love is very strange. Some people love with all they have: with their heart, eyes, hands, words. Others hide their love at the bottom of their souls and do not want the other to know anything about it at all—indeed, that love is so strange, not quite love but more like a shadow, a ghost; that's how your father loves me, but if we are afraid of our feelings, sooner or later they leave us or turn into something else. Drinking messed up your father, too; everything happened mostly because of his drinking, but what people do for a living certainly affects them, so the butcher's job messed up his head. But Tano does not believe me and sulks when I tell him that; he thinks that every job deserves respect. What if he were right? I think, son, that we two are also guilty because we did not try to understand the man, we made no attempt whatsoever but continued to loathe his job secretly, instead of telling him that directly; not that we could have changed anything, but at least he would have realized that it's not him that we despise. I wonder if you understand me. Every man keeps a spotless niche in his soul, almost like a piece of heaven. Do you know, say, how many songs your father knows? More than two hundred! Every time he sings he raises his face to the sky, because the song is a thing that raises a man's face up. And how does Tano remember those songs if not with his soul? He is not evil, believe me, son, and try to forgive if you haven't done it yet. Because forgiveness cures.

So many things I want to write to you about and I can't find the right words but, anyway, we are doing fine: your father doesn't touch grappa anymore, and I have new crutches, much more comfortable and, the most important, white as doves; I started growing a new sort of carnation and taught your father not to pee in their bed, and it looks like this is all for now.

Best regards from your mother, Zelma.

I'm looking at your photo, son, and I'm wondering why although you've grown so much, your eyes are still the same.

In the late fall of 1913, the first to meet the refugees was the Fisherwoman: they stand on the beach, their feet covered in fungi from the moisture, their faces grey with fatigue and strain; they stand looking at the sea, and it is infinite, and they could stand and look at it forever, as if enchanted.

They had finally dragged themselves, almost crawling, to Bulgaria and only now they begin to realize the stunning absurdity: Bulgaria is on this bank, but also where they left their villages: the border splits their land in two. There's hardly any country like Bulgaria, its border dividing it in two pieces, so it is both here and there, ours and foreign, and no whole can be made out of its two halves. In the region of Edirne, among the smoldering remains of another short and fearsome war, this time between the allies of the previous war, the Bulgarians left their homes, fields, memories, dreams; they ran away from them, dragging their feet through the dense Strandja woods, refugees from their own country and refugees in it, refugees from their own life.

It turns out that to be a refugee is mostly a feeling. The feeling of having a motherland is passed from generation to generation and the refugees here will pass to their offspring the feeling of lost motherland. The oldest of them, haunted by a thought, tries to share it hesitantly, even bashfully, "Well, when you think of it, it's simple; the motherland is where you have a roof over your head." But the young express their vehement disagreement, "The sky is the roof over all creatures' heads, but we can't say that the whole earth is our motherland!"

"And this is the mistake we made, this is it, this is how the human species was messed up," the old man mutters to himself now.

The young continue to look for the best place to build new nests for their children—like the swallows, they'd carry feathers and straw, mud and water under their tongues because they have nothing else to start building the future with. "The sea is the mother of the hungry," somebody mentioned casually and all agreed en bloc, "the sea is full of fish and there's always more." Only the old man dares to grumble, "The sea also needs ploughing and digging, you see," but they don't see again and head for the big water.

They stay on the beach, light fires and fuss around. *This is the place.* The Fisherwoman watches them from above. A small figure leaves the camp, skips on the stones, climbs up the slope, like a goatling she is, might have been raised in the mountains, the woman thinks about the girl who promptly reaches the top and gasping, stands on the edge of the abyss. "Wow, awesome," she marveled loudly looking at the Fisherwoman, and the woman smiled spontaneously, "Well, aren't you afraid?"

"Ha! Me—afraid! I grew up in the mountains; what hills I climbed there, with hilltops so high!"

The Fisherwoman enters the shack, takes from the cold grid a piece of grilled mackerel, puts it on a chunk of bread, gets out and slips it into her visitor's hands. "Gee!" the girl says, beaming, "It's been some time since I ate one of those!" Her talk is an odd mixture of Greek and scanty Bulgarian, "What are you, girl, Greek or Bulgarian?" The girl waves, "I have no idea what I am at all, I could be from anywhere, but my mother and father are Bulgarian." Waving her hands, rolling her eyes and beaming, she quickly tells her life. A child of Nature, the Fisherwoman thinks and sudden tenderness catches in her throat: glory to you, God, that you gave the children the gift to accept the trials and tribulation without objections, to live life as it is and know unawares that tribulations are inevitable. But the most important is, God, that so nonchalantly and magnanimously they forgive our sins, and when a child forgives the sins of an adult, it's as if you forgave them— and life is easier for all!

The girl comes very close, touches the Fisherwoman trustingly, silently thanks her. The woman looks in her eyes and flinches. The girl is not of the people who accept life without demur. The Fisherwoman keeps peeking behind the azure curtain of the girl's glance and sees: she is a fighter by nature, she has the strength to fight with life if necessary, fight it off tooth and nail because she believes that man can control fate, not surrender to its will, *contrary to the boy whom she is fated to meet.*

"Wow! Strong girl, you see."

The Fisherwoman stands still on top of the hill watching how the girl climbs down the slope. Every now and then the girl looks back and flashes a smile as bright as the sun. The Fisherwoman lets go, *come again sometime!* And wonders at the words coming from a forgotten niche in her soul.

ELADA PINYO'S FRIEND CONSIDERS IT IMPERATIVE TO INTERRUPT THE NARRATIVE WITH A BRIEF COMMENT

I closed the last page of Elada Pinyo's second notebook. If you remember it ends with Pinyo meeting her birth mother. That is all. I have to continue alone though, but it's getting increasingly harder because with time, Elada Pinyo becomes ghostlier in my memory, less and less material, somehow disembodied, just a memory of a voice, a glance of violet light, a memory of laughter, but memory is another reality, deviation from the truth; I am getting even more confused as I am switching between the two realities with ease; the twister, called Elada Pinyo, whirls even more and I give up, I refuse to be the co-author to the story of her life; I even think that I don't have the right to reach for the white sheet until I clarify for myself some simple things I don't understand, like: Is Elada Pinyo a child or a hundred year old woman, is she dead or alive, have I ever met her or will our paths cross in the future, could I tell in my own words what she told me herself without changing the meaning but, most importantly, will I have faith in my own skills because if you don't believe in yourself, you can't deal with other people's affairs since you can harm them, despite your good intentions.

I cowardly put away my notes, hide the paperback notebooks; I have no skill, no faith, no right. And then I remember the last day we were together; I don't want to, but I remember it as if somebody forced it on me, insisted, required: Elada Pinyo, shrunk under the years to a little bird, sat in the wicker chair like it were a big golden nest and she—a real bird with violet eyes, some shaggy fluff on top of her head, and nails as hard as the bird's legs; she was old, old, old, so old that she had started to turn into a child; I have two baby teeth, ma sheri, and I drink more and more milk; in fact, I can't eat anything else, my stomach rejects everything but milk. I smell like a baby now and I feel strange when I detect the scent myself; with age, I should smell of dust, of earth, you know, but no. I think it could be because I have actually drunk milk all my life but never enough, and, who knows, perhaps I'm simply going back.

The hundred-year-old asthmatic woman, wheezing, starts telling her unbelievable life; deep down in the backwoods, it was desolate and magnificent and she looks bravely into the eyes of a hundred year horror. Oh, God, we don't understand your divine design not because it is complex, but because it is too simple, so to grasp it, we lack faith; our heads burst with thinking, but faith does not accept reflections, not because they are reckless, but because faith is above any reflection. This is what John Chrysostom said and my experience confirms it because despite everything that went through my head, the books I read and Chrysostom people I met, yet I lack enough faith—that's how we all have been created. Nobody can teach you to have faith but the moment when faith just happens to you, all of it, at once. However, we also need to work on it because if God sees we are working on ourselves, he'll give us everything, everything we need and you will get faith, ma sheri, and stop reasoning because faith renders hopeless all anguish and reflections ...

And here, I am taking out again the notebooks with my notes and sinking into my memories to restore the living story of Elada Pinyo about her life in Burgas. I hope I can continue the story up to the point I am familiar with because, mysteriously, I have faith that I can still make the right words find me—then I will calmly accept the responsibility for what I am writing about.

The girl sits on the ground and through the slits in her half-closed eyelids observes the world around. Small, sad, pathetic world: an old man sitting in the sun at the low wall has turned the hem of his coat inside out and is trying to catch a flea; the flea hops, the old man gets irritated; a ginger cat stretches its back blissfully, its fine bones crack, the cat walks with wild, lurking steps through the sun-baked yard; the old man throws a stone at her and grins, the cat darts through the weeds to the neighboring yard and the girl yells angrily, "Don't you dare, stay away, I'm telling you!" The old man snickers and continues to rummage for the flea.

The girl sits in the shade of the quince tree, looks aimlessly at the run-down yard and sighs often, her sigh heavier than the yellow quince hanging above her head. "Why are you sighing?" the old man teases. He has caught the flea and is crushing it with the nails of his thick fingers, "Don't sigh now when you carry just a leaf on your shoulder, sigh when you carry the tree."

The girl looks under her eyebrows. Still sitting, the old man slides closer to her along the wall and starts picking his coat again. "Once upon a time, lassie, there lived two neighbors, one hardworking and rich, the other lazy and poor and they were on good terms with each other; once when the rich one headed for the woods to cut wood for the beams of a new house, the other joined him for company; they walked deep into the oak wood and the rich man cut a tree, rubbed his hands contentedly, put it on his shoulder unpruned and headed back to the village, dragging it behind. The other followed him and heard the neighbor moan and groan: the damn tree was heavy as if made of iron; the other felt guilty he was walking with no load and was of no help but since he was lazy, he picked a leaf from the tree, put it on his shoulder and started moaning and groaning like he carried a load too. So they entered the village bent to the ground—one with the tree, the other with the leaf. And the one behind with the leaf was moaning and groaning much more."

Then the old man looks straight into the girl's eyes,

"So, lassie, I'm telling you over and again: don't moan when you carry the leaf, time enough for that when you shoulder the tree."

The ripe quinces are hanging low and a faint, tart smell is coming from them. What a miracle a tree is with all those smells in it, the sap, fruits and seeds; maybe the soul of a tree is in a little seed, who knows? Once Syruie had explained to her why the trees are green, *they are alive, too, Pinyo; chlorophyll runs through them, the light green blood of the plants. Oh, Syruie ...*

A stone swishes past, the cat gives a shrill meow, the old man giggles leaning his head on the wall, all his gaping teeth exposed. "Funny, miserable, goofy geezer, you no good man," the girl screams in hysterics, gets up and goes to the backyard.

There the mother stands at the wooden hemp crusher, grips the handle tight and hits hard. The iron teeth break the hemp stalk with a crunch; from time to time, the woman throws a sheaf on the crusher, splinters from the hard bark fly around, and the tail of silvery hemp fiber twists, softer and more flexible. The mother puts all her passion in this simple job, wildly ramming away, in a frenzy. The girl is watching her. The woman senses her presence with her back. She stops, her head still bent, and her knuckles, clutching the handle, turn white.

The girl swings around and walks out to the road in front of the house. A sluggish gutter runs there, and the twins, the youngest members of the family, are squatting around it. Dirty and splashed with mud to the ears, they diligently knead dirt and water and arrange small male figurines along the gutter. "Are you making a new humankind, little brats," the old man teases, having moved closer. "Make it different then, very different! For God has made a mistake with us, whichever way you look at it!" The old man giggles in his palm, the twins throw slush in his face and laugh, too—the mirth is in full swing and it all looks like another sloppy job making the new men. But the old man sighs,

"Eeh, lassie!"

Suddenly he starts shaking all over, a tear trickling down from his eye, "Are we guilty or not, I still can't understand. See your mother's plight now; she won't dare look you in the eyes; when you found each other, her guilt came alive right before her eyes, a smiling, blue-eyed guilt, but it's scary to look her in the eyes. We left you there in the woods then because you were sickly and cried all the time and your cries could have betrayed the other children."

"I know," the girl cuts him off.

"You know nothing! Men on this earth are like refugees, by God's design! Their root is somewhere else, not on the earth, but where is the wretched root, I don't know! And this is why people are crippled, and your mother's soul is crippled so instead of being happy she found you, she withers under her guilt ...”

The girl feels guilty that her mother feels guilty. It's a vicious circle. The biggest quince thumps down from the branch to the ground. It's all rotten and smells sweet and fresh. The girl buries her nose in its mushy core and refuses to lift her face.

The old man gets up and shuffles through the refugee neighborhood, his dry cough fading away. And the girl, Pinyo, will go home in the afternoon languor, curl in the darkest corner of the house and wish to fall asleep in order to feel the immensity and magnificence of the miracle called dreaming, which has come to her quite recently after a long delay.

While she was living in Edirne, and earlier in the mountains, Pinyo never dreamed, or she might have dreamed but one of those deep, phantom dreams, which leave no memories. Here dreaming suddenly and truly happened to her and amazed, she realized that a dream can win over time with ease because it is a kind of reality in which things can happen again, though in a mysteriously complicated way. Pinyo was frightened in the beginning and could by no means understand how she could be here and there at the same time but gradually got used to it and stopped screaming the moment she woke up. One night she heard Syruie's voice and it was not a dream but a real, living voice: *Pinyooo, I am the universe now and it is wonderful to be the universe, Pinyo, to be in everything and all of it to be in you, just don't be sad and frightened; I'd like to tell you everything about myself, but now I can no longer be explained;* Pinyo's dream was a radiant mess of light, heady speed, shapeless objects floating in zero gravity and Syruie's voice, coming from somewhere, and another voice, quite near, interweaving with hers and uttering meaningless words seriously: *put more meat cracklings in the bread and milk, Maria;* a rooster strains its writhing throat in a fiery scream; the wind flaps wings of real silver, raises scattered splinters of hemp stalk and a cloud of hemp fiber; the longing for Syruie grows and curls into a sweet ball in the stomach; only the chaos in what is happening is real and Pinyo needs to create herself again out of the chaos and leave her dream in order to interpret it; everybody does that, dream and then interpret the dreams, but since people need inexplicable things as well, she won't leave this dream for anything in the world; she does not need to go back to the meaningful world if things can happen that way too.

However the rooster with the writhing throat frantically creates the morning, flaps mighty, fateful wings and brings to mind this meaningful and inevitable world, and reluctantly, Pinyo opens her eyes. Things were more real in her dream; Syruie's last words still ring in her ears, *nobody leaves your life because it's not possible,*

the living dream about the dead and the dead dream about the living and when it happens at the same time, they meet and you and I, Pinyo, we dreamed the same dream,

the rooster spews lava of ecstatic praise

and Pinyo was fully awake and started slurping the bread-and-milk with cracklings, *your mother slightly burnt them,* yummy bread and milk, with golden brown, crunchy cracklings; the morning was clear and Pinyo felt relieved the dream was gone because she felt the coming of a simple and clear day, which could be as real as her dream.

With time, Syruie started coming into her dreams more often. On the verge of sleep, she'd think *Syruie* and she'd appear, small and serious, wobbling her glass head and speaking her unchildish words. Pinyo was trying to call into her dream Hrisoula, Ovanes and Yorgos, but not even once did they respond to her wish; perhaps they failed to see themselves in their dreams at the same time Pinyo saw them so the dreams just missed each other, but it could be that what Syruie was talking about did not happen to the living; once Irinyo flashed by, uninvited, mumbled something quite indistinct and did not even stop, but stepped out of the dream right away.

One night the doe came. At last, Pinyo pressed her cheek against the doe's warm flank, smiled sadly and wept. She hadn't wept ever since she was a child. She was like a stream of tears that never stops; she wept, hugging the doe's neck. In her dream, she remembered Ovanes' words *man is seventy percent water, we are creatures of water* and now Pinyo was draining through her eyes; her water was turning into a stream which branched through all the cracks in the house, soaked the yard, watered the trees and they burst into leaves, but Pinyo was still draining and when all her water drained, she woke up amazed that her body was whole and unharmed. Syruie had drained like that, but forever. The inexplicable remained so and Pinyo completely agreed that people should not want to know every single thing; she was content she'd dreamed about the doe, that she had put her face to the doe's warm flank and that her dream was a chance to get back what she thought she had lost forever. Because wherever else but in the reefs of dreams could she meet the doe?

Who says that the mountain is frightening! The

mountain is full of trees, full of Hrisoula and the doe, and full of me forever. Wow! If I head straight now through the prickly bushes, brambles and rocks, I know I won't get lost. Some path will lead me and that's what I want so much! The urge to do it frightened her and she looked around.

They were in a sparse, bright wood. Her father is too far ahead and Pinyo's watching how he stamps in black the bark of some dry trees. Before that he's examined the tree from all sides, stroked its bark and pressed his ear against it to hear how the sap runs under. This one is sick. This will live a year or two. More black stamps appear because this wood is old and sick.

Her father started working as a forest ranger and she envied him with all her heart, "Gee, I want to be a guard of trees too!" Her father smiled, "They call it a forest ranger." Pinyo was stubborn, "Well, I want to be a guard of trees." She couldn't resist her longing for the mountain and her father took her with him to stamp dry trees. They arrived early in the morning in a horse-driven cart and Pinyo rushed to roam around as if she'd never done that before. Her skirt was all burs and thorns, her face was flushed, and her heart fluttered.

As she was watching her father's measured movements, she was suddenly terrified: he looked like an executioner. "He looks like an executioner," she repeated in French, and it sounded even more ominous,

"Heey! Aren't you the guard of trees! Why are you killing them?"

"They are withered, Elada, and no good. They will give those away to the refugees, for firewood ..."

"Don't excuse yourself, just don't! What if you make a

mistake and they kill a tree by mistake?”

Confused, her father was silent.

Silently, she started helping him. Her father was a forest ranger, which was not exactly tree keeper … “People are also branded like this, lassie, but their brandings do not show,” he said once and his voice shook. “Same as your mother, branded by her pain, the black sin she bears … stamped right in her soul …”

“Nothing bad happened to me, *on the contrary*,” Pinyo tries to explain once again, but her father waves dismissively, “Don’t you see? It happened to her! She had to save her other kids, the older—those who are now married and live separately … so with old Peter, they left you behind. And Pinyo recalled: deep down in the backwoods, it was desolate and magnificent. Then her mother’s words, spoken in a quiet trance, *forgive me, farewell, I can’t*. Time had stopped for her mother then, literally stopped, and Pinyo did not see how she could help it start again. I love mom. She loves me. Why is that not enough?

“What about you? Where were you then?”—a sudden thought that had not troubled her so far. Only now did she see her father’s absence at that moment.

“I was not in the village when they chased you away, Elada, I left after you with another group. I wouldn’t have left you there, I would have carried you through the wood myself, apart from the others … But, damn human fate, it has been ordained for each of us.”

In the evening, Elada boasted, “Today I stamped more trees than *dad*.” She uttered the word quite unawares, for the first time after they had found each other. The mother’s whole body trembled. The father wiped his eyes with his hands, and smiled wanly, "Quite so, quite so, dear, you pick up fast, that's why …"

Then the old man impatiently intervened,

"Why are you bragging about those stamps, lass, like the great clerk you were! And in French you can curse, huh … Our Elada stamps trees, so what!"

"I'm Pinyo, enough with this Elada! I'm not two people, not one more, just Pinyo …"

The old man pretended he hadn't heard,

"God also stamps people, with those round black stamps … sitting at a looong table, he scratches his lice with the right hand, stamps with the left; that is, he is left-handed. For each man, your Dear Old God stamps in black in his pocket book. Bang!—this one won't wait for tomorrow to come, a viper will nip his foot. Bang, here's another one—he'll come in a week's time; the flu will choke him, bad throat will finish you, man … Bang! Here's a stamp for you! As for you, a rusty nail will wipe you out—you see now, you survived three wars, one after another, a hurricane of bullets, thousands of bayonets did not harm you, a worthless nail did! But rusty! Because God stamps in black when the time comes, just like you and your dad. I just wonder lassie, why God acts like this: some people he takes too early, doesn't let them finish their work here … but others who are done with it and just hang out in the wide world, why does he still keep them here? Like say, he'll stamp me when I'm too old— doesn't he see I'm of no use to myself and the others? I curse him sometimes, the reason he still keeps me here: in other words, it's like, look how magnanimous I am, I'm the Lord and I do whatever I want and old Peter will get the longest life to burden and bore him so the damn old geezer understands that a life that's too long is a punishment equal to premature death. That's what I think, Elada, but God will judge if I'm right when we meet ..."

"Gee, if Syruie hears you, grandpa Peter, if she just somehow hears you, I don't know what'll happen to you! I really don't!"

One day in winter, the father was getting ready to take a dozen city leaders hunting. Pinyo sprang up, her eyes sparkling, "I'm coming, too." Old Peter objected, "Crazy girl, have you ever seen or heard a girl go hunting with the men! Sit tight on your butt and don't budge, is that clear, Elada!"

"If Elada so desires, she can stay, but I am Pinyo and I'm going!" She tossed her bluish-black braid from one shoulder to the other and flew around the house, packing up; the mother said nothing, the father didn't dare object and Pinyo jumped into the cart wrapped in her father's woolen, hooded cloak. In the other carts, the hunters shouted excitedly at each other, joked, rolled cigarettes, cracked flint lighters and drew in the smoke, furiously moving the cigarettes between their lips.

Feverish with anticipation, Pinyo stomps her feet, urges the horse, geee, her voice vibrates in the frosty morning.

They were going to shoot waterfowl along the shore and woodcocks at the foot of the mountain. Within an hour they were on the shores of Otmanliy, seething with waterfowl; as if it had been expecting them, the sun sailed out of the icy cold sea water; the frosty air cracked with fiery sparks that instantly flew to the sky and made the snow pink; seagulls screeched, dogs barked ferociously; a lively fuss ensued. The men scattered among the rocks; their rifles crackled frequently, their barrels smoked and fearful wings swished in the air. This is killing, thought Pinyo and, surprised, repeated: yes, killing, and I am happy; gee, isn't that what the waterfowl is for? She dashed after her father, screaming joyfully and he gestured to warn her not to make any noise.

Then they walked into a vast wood. The sound of the sea remained far away, silence lay on the laden tree twigs, squirrels scattered snow dust; shot, the woodcocks thumped in the snowdrifts and only then exhaled. Pinyo picked them up and hung them on her belt. Overexcited with the hunting and the crisp day, she sat in a cushion of snow on a log and quietly chuckled; the hunters squatted, leaned on the tree trunks, passed around a shiny bottle, sipped and wrinkled their noses; Pinyo heard them saying, "It's in this wood for sure, we'll close in on it, can't go anywhere." Her father, the forest ranger, was blinking somehow uneasily and mopping with a square linen kerchief his bald head, suddenly turned pink, "But … you know, it's prohibited, you know, the law …," but the men laughed, "We are the law."

The silence behind their backs feels heavy. The wood sighs. Filled with anticipation, Pinyo sways. A sudden force puts her on her feet and pushes her to walk through the snow, knee-deep in the snowdrifts. She walks without direction and her heart thumps, her temples pulse, the dead birds hanging on her belt hit her knees. She walks for a long time to the heart of the silence and stops in the middle of a round field; she listens and looks around. Her nostrils flutter, close, open, and smell something so familiar but she can't remember what it is; her heart now throbbing in her throat, she breathes in fitfully, weary of the closeness of that thing.

And then she saw her.

She had turned white all over, not from the snow but from age. Her nostrils fluttered like frosty brown leaves, and warm jets of breath came out of her half-open mouth. Her slanting, slightly bulging eyes met the girl's stunned glance.

"Oh, God!"

They stood like that forever, afraid to stir. Feeling for the first time that time can stop, Pinyo gripped her throat and it even occurred to her that time had never run, that this vast infinity had been here forever, frozen magnificently around. Something that had no name was happening; Pinyo at least could not name it; it was stronger than the sun, than the infinite silence, than the air and water, than the beating of her heart in all the veins of her body. Then the times were alive again; concentric circles of unspecified threat were coming from somewhere and they both were in their very center; Pinyo sensed their invisible web wrapping around them. At that moment the barking of a dog broke the silence and the doe winced, but somehow was in no hurry to run; Pinyo came to her senses and started waving her hands in panic, "Run, go away, hide, please!"; the doe was still there, her glance was turning even more human and that glance made Pinyo tremble all over. The sense of a coming threat was turning into something else that had no name either; the girl sensed its inevitability, tried to get ahead of it, and dashed through the snow, her feet wading deep, the frozen woodcocks hitting her knees; she unhooked them and threw them away; reaching the doe at last, she kneeled in the snow, rested her forehead against the doe's warm flank and immediately started pushing her, "Go away, please, please!"; the doe wearily closed her frosty eyelids and then the shot hit.

"Didn't I tell you, Elada, a girl should not go hunting; it brings bad luck, but you … you could have been killed, that's your second chance at life now!" "Third," the girl corrected the old man. Looking through the window with wide open eyes, the mother was wringing her hands with wan fingers; the father was panting and wiping his face with a square kerchief. Pinyo clenched her fists, the blood in her veins turned black, her pupils turned black and her lips turned as black as elderberries,

"That's my mother you killed!"

Silence fell in the room and Pinyo feared the echo of her words. As if a cold blade flashed in the twilight and she thrust it right in the delicate back of the woman at the window, a blade, coated with the poisonous spread of cold blooded revenge.

She jumped up, ran outside, and walked the narrow streets of the neighborhood for a long time. In the houses they were already lighting the gas pots and candles; the flickering lights enlarged and deformed the shadows of people on the curtains and the rooms seemed haunted. She walked to and fro on the dirty snow and then went back and sat on the steps to the gate. Old Peter stepped out, stood in the yard, lingered for a while and raised his head to the sky,

"So many stars, a veritable marvel; what if up there, on that star yonder, what if another old man like me sat there and what if he was also looking my way, towards our star."

Pinyo did not respond and the old man coughed,

"They say the earth is round and a star in the sky as teacher Stamenov told me once, but can you imagine that? It's damn unlikely! Although he was a teacher, I did not believe him; if the earth were a ball, how come we don't fall off, I asked, but he explained that we had roots like the trees, only invisible and infinite these roots were, thus letting us move wherever we wanted, so to say. Gravity, their name was or something like that."

Pinyo smiled in the darkness. She had read about the earth's pull in one of Syruie's books.

"What I want to tell you, granddaughter, is that it is very strange God's taken pains to create all this, but we don't intend to respect his work at all. Just imagine, he created a star to be our home, but we tore away pieces of this home to live in tribes and kill each other, steal land from each other and what not. Alas! To live on a star and not be aware of that!"

The old man paused and both heard how in the house one of the twins cried in his sleep, somewhere at the other end of the neighborhood a stray cat meowed, and the night turned even darker because other stars were rising in the sky.

"Look, lassie, she might not have been the same but quite different, not yours, eh? So many years have passed since … And that wood was different, far from here; why think she's come for you here, to this wood?"

The old man's voice grew thinner and broke.

Pinyo rose, opened the door noiselessly and entered the dark house. Old Peter lingered a while, hesitated, then waved at the faraway star, "God bless, old man." He brushed the snow off his feet and followed her.

It was on a late spring evening, a little before midnight, when Naked Ana appeared. The people had gone to bed and not a single light was in the windows, except the anxious light of the low full moon shining over the world.

Some had already met her on the streets in the neighborhood and had told the rest, so Pinyo's curiosity was riled by the incredible details, and that evening Ana herself had come from the distant edge of the swamp, from the butcher's shop. First they heard her loud, crystal clear voice singing one of her moon songs; only in full moon did she pace the streets. The song was a mess of words with almost no meaning, but cool, sad and beautiful in a peculiar way. Pinyo felt her hair bristle and wiggle. "Ohh, God, dear Goood, the sun rose and so did the moon; they both shine in the sky and the sea is all fish and the fish will drink it million years ago; a tree is blooming in the sea, all naked sea, all naked, oh, my poor tree, oh my poooor." The last word has no end; a round, piercing OH vibrates in the sky heading towards something infinitely distant, turns into a wail, a prayer for mercy, a protest, a dark moan, all these at the same time and it does not want to end. The Naked has no power to stop it, to prevent it from getting out of her depths; she paced the streets and the dogs howled with her; the moon shone on her naked body, her lemony yellow skin and fragile limbs; the tail of her sick song twisted above her head and the people stood behind the curtains as if bewitched and could not take their eyes off the sight, "Tell me about her, grandpa,"

"Why do you want to know, Elada; the other people's pain won't let up; Well, it happened at the time of the first refugees; when we left you in the cradle, at the same time, brigands attacked their group; Ana was fifteen then and walked with her family, eight–ten folks." Pinyo listens with her eyes wide open, shuddering in anticipation of the shock: one night Ana walked away from the group, too deep in the wood to do her business and as she was squatting and the cool moon was shining over her head, she heard in the quiet of the night horrific screams and cries coming from the direction where her family was. Shivering all over, Ana quickly slid into a hollow of an old tree, buried her face in her knees and plugged her fingers into her ears. When the screams stopped and everything was dead silent, Ana was still sitting in the hollow shivering; then the moon dripped white, the wood moved and the trees walked, stepping like silent giants, so Ana thought she must have been dreaming: it looked more like a dream to her; she stepped out from inside the tree, moved her stiff limbs and walked straight through the moonlight spots on the path; before long, she reached the camp but they were all asleep, motionless; Ana quickly slid next to her sister and then she sensed something was wrong; in the moonlight she saw them sleeping with their eyes open, empty, distant eyes but the most distant were her sister's eyes; "Come back," Ana asked her, "I beg you to come back; what are you all up to, don't scare me like that!" The luggage was scattered around and in the moonlit midnight, Ana was falling even deeper into this dream; frozen inside, but hurrying on the outside, she then closed their eyes and got down to work: she pulled them by the shoulders and dragged them through the bushes to the nearby dry gully, where she placed them next to each other, with her sister last; she sat and looked at her, talked to her monotonously and persuasively; "You were right," she urged and coaxed, because before this befell them, they had argued over a trifle; mad and forced to keep quiet, they had hissed like snakes at each other; "I hate you," Ana had whispered and even slapped her sister's fingers and no way she could forget that, make it go back; the slap just stayed there, on the little girl's hand and Ana gently took this hand in her hands and started stroking it guiltily, "Look now, I love you, I'm all love, nothing else happened, it was a trifle, but love is forever, love is; you see, I even forgot why we argued, come back now, come back and I'll change all over, I'll even change my name if you want. My name will be Love starting today, only Love, just forgive me and forget about the hatred, please, my little one, come back."

She stopped to rest, lifted her head and looked at the moon; she might have thought she saw people up there, kind of small and busy; God, where were they running to? Then Ana saw a knife glisten in the moonlight, a big curved knife, strange and scary, but she reached out and took it; she managed to dig the earth on both sides of the dry gully with it; her eyes closed tight, like a mole she dug; the soil was loose and fell lightly on her people, a soft and warm wrap around them, and when she finished at last, the moon had hid and morning mist drizzled; in the daylight, Ana saw her hands smeared with something dark and sticky, wet and sticky as her face and her heavy, sickly-smelling skirts were plastered to her body.

At last, Ana managed to utter, Loooord; she repeated it twice, thrice, and then she cut her clothes with the sharp knife, squeamishly pulled them down, tread furiously on them, lay naked in the wet grass and rolled down the slope and climbed up and did it again and again; she wiped her hands and face with a handful of leaves and rolled again, unaware that her skin was changing color, emitting a greenish radiance. In the end she sat in the grass and felt silence surging from all directions, with no beginning or end, and only now was Ana really scared because she did not know how she could get out of this dream, but she had to somehow defend herself from the deadly silence that filled it, so she started singing in a low, trembling voice; she couldn't unglue her lips, so initially she sang with her belly, but gradually her voice gained confidence and sudden power; clear and lucid like glass, it found its way up among the trees and towards the heavy, unresponsive sky. Ana sang all the songs she knew and when she was done, she went on singing the words she knew in random order until her voice was hoarse.

That's how other refugees, hiding from the brigands in the same wood, found her; they heard her songs from a distance, followed the sound and saw her sitting naked in the grass, her back strictly straight; in the daylight her skin was as pale as a crocus and glistened from the dew, her eyes were closed and her mouth poured a word without end:

"Looooord!"

The thought of Naked Ana replaces the thought of the doe's death; Pinyo can't stop imagining everything that had happened to this strange woman and especially, Ana holding her sister's dead hand. "Loooooord," Pinyo draws out involuntarily and shudders, and Pinyo suspects that Naked Ana is not by chance in this town; people like her are never by chance anywhere but why, the girl doesn't know; she just so wants to meet the Naked one day and look into her eyes, look through her eyes and find an answer to the question why Ana is not a chance encounter in this town, for Pinyo either, and one day she meets her and looks into the abyss of Ana's eyes.

It was a dazzling day in spring and the Poultry Market beat wings, cackled throatily, crowed; fluff and feathers floated in the air, and it was merrier than ever. Pinyo walked aimlessly and peeked curiously into the bird cages where canaries were chirping and parrots snorting; she teased the peasant women, louder than the birds they held tightly by the legs. She stopped to see the black rooster, watching her with fury in his yellow eye. Pinyo hadn't seen a wilder one and stepped back; wow, the rooster shook its comb, snapped its beak and was just about to fly out of the hands of the sturdy peasant woman, who fought with him, pushed down his head and tucked it under one wing. The savage relaxed and fell asleep right away; Pinyo winked at the woman and smiled.

And right at that moment a cry rose from the crowd, aaaaaa came out of many mouths at the same time; the birds stopped swishing their wings, the pigeons in the cages hushed their cooing, even the hens stopped cackling and in the sudden silence, Pinyo looked where everybody did. Naked Ana was walking in the crowd, stark naked; in the daylight, her skin had the pale color of a real crocus; she was skinny with hands like sticks and thighs long and narrow; the pubic bone above them was covered with light greenish fluff; even more greenish was the fluff showing out of her armpits; her breasts were tender, hardly noticeable like in an immature girl, but her face looked so aged that at first Pinyo placed her at well above forty.

The naked woman walked without stopping anywhere; she hurried past the cages with parrots, pigeons and canaries without looking at them; she was walking towards something only she saw, something that was always running a step before her, and she just kept following in its tracks and then she suddenly stopped, stopped right in front of Pinyo.

Right into her eyes stared Naked Ana and the girl froze, closed her eyelids tight with all her might and felt how Ana reached out, caught her hand and locked it within hers. When Pinyo opened her eyes and looked into Ana's, something was coming back in them from a place very far away; her pupils were changing their color, the swampy green was getting clearer and they shone with a verdant light; oh, the Naked woman smiled sympathetically and started stroking the girl's fingers; ohhh, her icy fingers were getting warmer and Pinyo felt their warmth pouring into her; ohhh, Naked Ana uttered tenderly and compassionately and did not stop caressing with her thin fingers,

"It's all right, it's aaall right," all the tenderness in the world in these fingers, all the love in the world in these eyes,

Sunk to their bottom, Pinyo wept,

"Don't cry, now, nothing happened, it's all right."

"Only love, now, only love, love like this, soooo big as the sky, see?" and Ana opened her hands wide to show her love

and then, an old woman tossed a cheesecloth on her shoulders, "It's a shame, folks, if she does not understand, don't we all see? It's a sin to walk naked."

Ana suddenly shuddered, her eyes grew dark, her

hands-cold; she dropped Pinyo's hand, wriggled her shoulders squeamishly and threw the cheesecloth off, noooo; it fell in the dust and the Naked ran to the green spot of kale next to the nearby fence, tore some leaves and started feverishly rubbing her hands, face, body and kept rubbing until the leaves turned into green mush; clean all over again, Ana walked away with her drawn-out, indignant oooh, but it had no color, no strength anymore; the surge of love had passed and the Naked did not turn even once to look at Pinyo, nor anybody else; she went down the street towards the swamp and at last, the women started to cross themselves, the roosters crowed and they all forgot Naked Ana; only Pinyo ran home, stumbling and gasping for breath …

This was in the spring, but on a quiet morning at the end of the summer Pinyo heard that Naked Ana had attacked Tano, the butcher.

The people in the neighborhood talked agitatedly about that and wondered how it could happen. Barring her surges of tenderness and compassion, Ana was quiet and did not bother anybody, but the prentice at the butcher's shop dropped a few hints and everything became clear.

She left the refugees' house at the swamp where she lived and ambled away; she walked, smiled and looked nobody in the eyes though she met a lot of people on her way; an old woman cursed her dismissively, another woman shook her head compassionately, some children screamed cheerfully after her, "Ana the Naked, Nakeeed Anaa;" one man crossed himself, "Oh child, child," but Ana did not look at them; she went straight into the butcher's yard, where she hadn't been yet, climbed straight upstairs, saw Zelma, approached her bed, sat at her feet and started stroking her hand; she stroked it for long, until the swampy green in her pupils cleared to grassy green, light green, tenderness and longing. Then for the first time she allowed somebody to stroke her hands, "Love eeh, all of them, eeh …" and Zelma reached out, picked a scarlet geranium and gave it to her; Naked Ana beamed and put it in her hair, stopped at the threshold, beamed even more and pattered down the stairs; Zelma neither heard, nor saw how Ana entered Tano's butchery; she did it noiselessly and startled the man, facing him with a big smile on her face; naked and pitiful like a big chicken just gotten out of its egg, she started stroking his hand without any hesitation. Tano smiled, confused, and drew back but quickly came to his senses and listened to Ana's chatter; what did this girl, this not-yet-woman want from him, what did her fingers want and her empty, shadowy eyes, what did her low, soft voice want; love, yes, love but Tano did not understand she did not want, but gave love and that was his mistake; it occurred to him that he hadn't touched a woman since that thing happened with Zelma; somehow he did not dare touch his wife yet though a long time had passed and this nestling here was not that ugly; her eyes were a bit empty, but that was all.

"Love, love," the man repeated, "nice love I'll give you; it'll do you good," he talked to her as if she'd understand him better if he distorted his words, "wait a minute," shaking, he pushed her hand and wiped the table with his palm and that was his other mistake; he drew Ana close, fondled her puny breast and lifting her under the hips, lay her on the table; Ana tried to get up, protracting an offended and reproachful ooooh, but Tano did not hear anything, "Your skin is soft and moist like silt, girl, what kind of skin is this?" Ooh, she tried to push him with her hands, but the table was already creaking and then Zelma heard the girl's scream; at the same time the man knew; "Well, well, then, why did you beg me then? Get up, let's go home, come on." Upstairs Zelma got up on her crutches, reached the stairs and to go faster, sat and slid down. Tano apologetically touched Naked Ana, "It's nothing, nothing happened; just go," but she saw his palm, smeared with something sticky and shuddered all over; with this palm he tried to stroke her face so her crocus-colored skin felt wet and sticky; terrified, Ana saw the knife, big, strange and scary, with a dark, sticky edge, just like that other one, perfectly the same; her strong fingers gripped it, and when Zelma finally dragged herself to the butchery, it was too late.

The apprentice heard and saw all that when he came back unexpectedly and before he decided to interfere, ("After all, Tano's my master") he saw her head towards the old walnut tree, slide into its hollow, bury her face in her knees and shake all over, while Zelma was shouting from the butchery …

… Ana stopped making her impetuous walks on the streets. Her bouts ceased and the green swamp of her eyes grew thicker: the slightest noise made her shake continuously. The police were looking for a suitable place for her and finally decided to settle her in an obscure village in the Strandja mountain because down here she could be dangerous. She had ripped up Tano the butcher who lay barely alive in the clinic without hopes for any future and all that because Naked Ana got sudden bouts of love, which could not always be prevented and because her lonely, naked songs at night stirred the thrilling memory of things that people wanted to forget once and for all.

So one morning a uniformed policeman entered the yard of the house where Ana lived and soon a crowd of curious people gathered; the policeman was shifting his feet, "Come on, have her dressed," and he handed a bundle of clothes to the hostess; she hesitated with the bundle in hand and when she went in, they heard how Ana screamed as the woman was trying to say something reassuring; then the door opened and the Naked flew out, ran to the hedge and squatted there, shaking like a skinny chicken, greener than usual, noooo; other women entered and started helping, but Ana sprang up and ran around the yard; they ran after her but couldn't catch her and dust was rising up, and suddenly, Ana rolled her eyes and dropped to the ground. The women gathered around her, hurriedly clothed her, gave her a few slaps and brought her to her senses.

And here she is, Naked Ana, dressed in a new skirt, headscarf around her head and terror in her eyes; noooo, she tries to tear her skirt, but just short of rips off the lace edging on her chest; ooow, she pulls off the scarlet headscarf and squeezing it tight in her fingers, clutches it impulsively to her chest; the policeman gives her a push in the back, "Make sure she doesn't snatch the gun and shoot you too," they tease him, "and don't you dare get under her skirt, 'cuz she'll shoot and won't think twice about it!"

Here comes the Fisherwoman, back from the fish market with a small, empty basket on her shoulder; she's heard everything about Ana; she stands there and looks under her eyebrows, thinking slowly and heavily, then takes Ana's hand and leads her through the crowd.

The policeman looks after them, but the Fisherwoman does not turn back, *the human species is the lowest of all creatures on earth;* "What did you say, Fisherwoman?" the policeman asks, confused. "Nothing, whoever heard, they did; whoever didn't, it doesn't matter," the woman mutters, the policeman shuffles towards the precinct to report the situation and the neighborhood calms down fast.

ABOUT THE TIME WHEN AT LAST PINYO MET DAVID AND DAVID MET PINYO

Pinyo skips around in a girlish way, her skirts swinging like a blue bell. She is going to the town center to watch how Ferso kneads Easter cake in the pastry shop, to breathe the warm, dizzying air, fragrant with the scent of vanilla and marmalade, to laugh with Ferso for no reason at all and get even prettier with the anticipation of the coming holiday; the holiday really transforms people but why that is so, Pinyo doesn't know; she just prances around and her skirt swings and shows now and then her bare legs like exquisite gas lamp shades, thin at the ankles but with rounded calves; the slippers flop on the stones and the girl rushes to get ahead of the sound of her own footsteps, her hair swinging on her back, her prickly breasts bouncing in the bosom of her shirt and her whole body in a flutter.

"Slow down, don't fly away," a strong hand stops her, "those who fly could fall from up high," Miron the docker smiles in her very face; the scent of barber cologne and freshly ironed clothes drifts towards her mixed with the smell of something else she can't place, but that scent precisely stuns her and she is not in a hurry to pull her hand out of the pliers of Miron's hands; for a moment her glance sinks in the reefs of Miron's look, she feels weak under the ribs, a hot flame licks her low belly and her legs turn soft, but she gathers all her strength, pulls her hand back in panic and darts away, afraid she'd slump at this man's feet. "Eheey, you, winged creature," Miron laughs after her, but Pinyo does not turn back; she's deadly scared by what had singed her body in seconds; she does not know what to call it, but it reminds her of something long-forgotten, of the Karakachan's cabin, where Yorgos gasps and Hrisoula whispers her husky, timeless words while their naked bodies rub against each other, blue sparks fly around and the air could blaze up any minute.

Terrified, Pinyo stops running: what was that, what?

"Is a dragon chasing you?" Ferso distracts her from the unexpected thoughts. She stands at the door of the pastry shop and smiles with her dimples, with the blue pupils of her slanting eyes she smiles and touches her with a white hand, and Pinyo feels with relief how the thrill of Ferso's touch relaxes her belly muscles. The air in the shop truly intoxicates with the scent of vanilla and apricot jam; Pinyo smiles and then they both burst out laughing; laughter with no reason is the youngest feeling in the world, happiness with no reason is their inner sky; the feast runs in their bodies' veins, sparkles in their eyes; they can't stop laughing and it feels light and sweet to breathe in the shop, to feel, to forget, to remember; it's even dangerous sometimes, but why so, Pinyo wouldn't know, "Come on, that's enough! I'm spent, Ferso."

On the way back, Pinyo walks tamed, light shines on her forehead, the bell of her skirt sways close to her ankles and her hair's calm on her shoulders.

"Heey, you, winged creature, you've had a wonderful time, eh?!"

Miron stands at the entrance to the refugee neighborhood and stares arrogantly into her eyes; her head cocked, Pinyo tries to walk proudly past him; how independent Pinyo is, how inaccessible, but the docker grabs her wrist and the scent of a slightly stale cologne and of that other thing wafts towards her, but now it turns her off with its heavy energy—the girl staggers and tries to pull her hand out of the clasp of his hands, "Only if I let you; only I can let you out of the cage, golden bird." Pinyo hides her hand behind her back and feels the painful bracelet around her wrist, "You have no right, who do you think you are!" she snarls from a distance and the docker laughs throatily,

"Well done, Elada! Good girl, you're my match!" Pinyo walks away feeling the thrusts of male arrogance behind her and suddenly grasps that in some extraordinary way the man laughing behind will try to steer her life, interfering fatefully and inevitably.

One day her nostrils fluttered like a doe's. She felt unbearably restless and festive and was on the streets again: have a good day, hello, smiles, prancing, happiness for no reason; when she reached the main street, she was greeting even strangers defiantly; close to the harbor at the end of the street, she stopped at the main entrance of Hotel Imperial, took a deep breath and looked around: boys blacker than shoeshine shout; seagulls caw and squeak; a half torn poster whips the wall of the hotel. Pinyo's throat is dry, her heart is pounding, but nothing happens, "Eheey, it's too early for you to hang around the Imperial, too young for that kinda job, eh?" hurrying dockers tease her, laugh loudly and walk away.

"What are you doing here, Elada?! March back home!" Really angry, Miron pulls her by the sleeve and pushes her in the back to move, "I forbid you to hang around here," he pushes her again and catching up with the other porters, looks back several times, gloomy like a rain cloud.

Pinyo swung around and walked the road home deep in thought; her sense of smell had misled her for the first time; perhaps, her gift to distinguish scents was leaving her, but then, her nostrils fluttered again as she smelled something tart, not too distant and overwhelming, even dizzying. She was mad at her own inability to determine its direction but she knew that it was happening here, in Burgas, so she could let it happen without her help if only she didn't feel that the event concerned her more than any other person in the town. So she almost raced to the main street again and found herself at the same place near the harbor; leaning against the hotel's wall, she felt almost like crying because somebody was making fun of her forcing her to run the streets like crazy, without knowing why she was doing it; on the wall next to her, a poster was whipping against the wall and annoyed, she tore it, crunched it into a ball in her fist and ran back home.

"Pina Peachina," the twins were making faces at her and showing their tongues; she hit one with the paper ball she was still grasping in her fist; the boys smoothed the paper, rolled it out on the floor, pushing each other furiously and read with difficulty, "Charitable … coooncert … for refugees." Pinyo pulled the paper out of their hands, buried her face in it and inhaled the smell of printing ink: here it was!

In the evening the hall of the Thrace Movie Theatre was bursting at the seams; the standees had almost climbed one on top the other; big gas lamps were burning on the walls and the smell of coal gas mixed with the aroma of Turkish coffee, which servers carried on shiny trays high above their heads; they served only the audience in the first row, the city leaders.

Pinyo was sitting between her mother and father. Her cheeks were burning, her nostrils never stopped fluttering.

Her gift to distinguish scents had improved so much that it led her to the poster soaked in fresh printing ink; the letters written on this poster carried some message that she hadn't grasped until this moment, but she sensed that tonight, in this hall, she would see a sign.

First all present sang about the clear moon rising over the Strandja wood; tears were rolling down the faces of most; it was a very touching spectacle, Pinyo pondered, all this human mass which sang crying or cried singing; then they all noisily took their seats and stared at the stage. The actors appeared, sang folk songs, hopped in ruchenica and horo, showed folk traditions from Edirne and played the bagpipe. The audience was fully caught up in the performance.

Finally a young man came out, dressed in black, European clothes. Pinyo's fingers gripped the back of the chair in front of her. They announced that the man had come from Spain and that he was a very famous mime in a big city there, Madrid; the audience had no idea what that thing could be but applauded him heartily and voiced their surprise when told that he was born here, in Burgas. Then a whisper floated through the hall and many eyes focused on the first row, where a comely woman was sitting, a cloud of fluffy hair around her head; the woman was constantly pulling at the lace collar of her dress, trying to straighten it; a pair of white crutches leaned against her chair.

The servers turned off all lamps and in the ensuing darkness, the flames of tall candles shone from the enormous candle holders in front of the stage. The man closed his eyes and the candlelight lit up his face. Music drifted into the room; a lonely violin was playing somewhere behind the curtain and the man was listening to it in no hurry; he stood like this for a long time and when he finally opened his eyes, it was clear that somehow he had forgotten all those people in the hall. Pinyo felt this and bristled with anticipation. The man tossed back his head, then abruptly scooped all the sky with his hands and rising on tiptoes, flew up in the sky he had created with a single gesture. His long fair hair fluttered in the wind, his body was swinging impetuously, as if moving in all directions at the same time, his hands scooped with all their might, the wide silk sleeves of his shirt flapped like real wings and the flames of the candles glowed like distant stars. Pinyo's teeth were chattering and she could swear that right before her eyes the man was really flying. She clasped her hands together so they wouldn't shake. That was it. A man appeared, strange and lonely; he had gone beyond spaces and centuries and overcome thousands of dark moments; his name had appeared on a poster with the smell of printing ink, a poster written by fate, and Pinyo had walked up to that poster in a trance to realize that among the men in this world this particular one existed, a stranger, but so scary close that she was ready even at this very minute to rush to the stage, look into his eyes, sick with longing, lead him away from here and tell him along the way about loneliness as big as the sky, which had also lifted her once high up with the stars, deep down there in the backwoods. Pinyo cried, not aware of the rising rumble of voices from the audience, craving spectacles, "Come on, that's enough, the boy ran around a bit, nice, but bring the gypsy, Hyacintha, to twist a belly dance for the soul, come ooon …"

"He was really flying, didn't you see, he was flying!"

On her way back, Pinyo was swinging her arms in a somewhat peculiar way. "Didn't you see for yourself?!" She got no reply, only old Peter mumbled hesitantly, "They say his mother, Jewish Zelma, once flew from the roof of the synagogue and hovered over Burgas for two hours, but I did not see her myself, so I don't know." "Crazy old man," the twins mocked him and he shut up.

Pinyo did not say anything either.

The golden dawn is tinged with red. At the window, Pinyo yawns and leans her forehead against the windowpane. Somehow she knows that what she sees first today will be of vital importance.

The streets are deserted. Crooked streets, all the same, as if taken from fairytales about dwarves, the same view of this Burgas suburb for six years. Pinyo stands behind the curtain, watching and waiting. At last, a man and a woman appear and stop in the middle of the street, with their backs to the house. Every hair on the woman's head shines like a beam of sunlight and the girl senses that the morning will be nice. It's Zelma, hanging on her white crutches, looking into the young man's eyes, rapt. Pinyo's heart skips a beat. His hands are still fluttering, his fingers are long and restless; with the help of these hands, he pulls the words out of himself, silent, sudden words. Drawn by their elegant dance, the girl stood agape. The deaf-mutes' language is more beautiful than French, Greek, or the language of the running water, even than the language of the doves. The man paused and Zelma's hands started talking; her bare hands dive in the air like big white fish, clumsily and hesitantly, so the man watches them intently.

Pinyo observes the scene in utter silence. The world is

really silent at this moment: the seagulls are not there, the doves have flown away, no sounds of people or any other noise. In the middle of this speechless world, the girl is speechless too, staring frankly at both of them. The man senses the stare, turns around and their eyes meet. Pinyo draws the curtain and her heart rings like a bell in her own ears. She is in the room, listening to herself.

Then she slid on some slippers, went out to the street and faced the man. She looked into his eyes, "It's me. Didn't you recognize me?" The man was watching silently. "I was at the theatre last night and saw you fly, I saw everything," She was trembling all over. Zelma put her hand on Pinyo's and asked quietly, "Talk to each other, you two. He is not deaf-mute, you'll see that yourself, Pinyo." She moved away noiselessly on her crutches, waving them like wings.

They remained there, still facing each other.

Pinyo was looking straight at him: his high forehead, dark serious eyes, sensuous mouth; he looks so much like somebody she knows, but she can't remember whom. He is also studying her closely: her extraordinary face with the hard, high cheekbones, the dimple on the chin, the bluish black hair combed behind the ears and her eyes so bright that the hint of something primitive, roughly-hewn in the girl's behavior seems of no consequence: hers is the most extraordinary face he has ever seen.

"I know, you look like Syruie! Wow, you really look like her! There, in your sky I mean, there's a Syruie; eight years ago she turned into white water and drained out, it's true; sometimes we both dream of each other at the same time; I here, she—from over there and we talk, I'm not lying … But I knew you are not by chance because fate pointed at you on a poster and I found you by myself.

I know who you are, so what if we don't know each other, I know everything about you, but I can't express it in words. Gee, how did all this happen, I wonder!"

They walk next to each other slowly, aimlessly. At last, they reach the sea. "You see, all roads lead to the sea; why did God make so much water but all salty ... it could be his tears, what if God weeps like men do ... Does God have something to weep for, eh?"

The man smiles.

She remembers she doesn't know his name and asks him; he catches a seagull's feather floating in the air, smoothes the sand with his palm and writes, David. Pinyo also writes her two names Elada Pinyo, "I don't know if I'd ever feel like Elada; I so want to make my mother happy and let people call me Elada because it's my birth name, but I'm Pinyo from head to toe, so I don't know ..."

They are walking on the black sand, seashells crunching under their feet, seagulls fluttering over their heads, fishing boats sailing into the sea and the day palpable, soaked in liveliness; Pinyo is part of it because waves like sea waves splash in her but only she senses them; her face has turned pink, her eyes sparkle, she can't stop talking; she wants to tell all of herself from the scarlet apron swing to today, to tell her whole story, but she cannot find enough words, she just can't; somehow, they scatter away; it must be because she talks for both of them, "I love the mountain so much, the sea scares me a bit; I love Hrisoula, linden tea and to watch how sparks fly from the burning log in the fire; I like to drink raw milk in the mountains, I drank it straight from the sheep's udder, and I like to dream about Syruie, to think about Ovanes, to touch mom's scared hands and to call her mom in my mind, and Naked Ana I love a lot, but they drove her away, because of your father, you know ..."

Embarrassed, Pinyo put her hand over her mouth. David said nothing, didn't even flinch, and pointed at a rock. They sat there, silently stared into the blue distance, and Pinyo felt a sudden relief in being silent with him to infinity because he was silent like the sea, the sky, the mountain. Words don't work so much if silence is more meaningful than them.

For a long time, nobody knew about their early walks. Pinyo slipped away unnoticed until one day she ran into old Peter. He was squatting in the burdock, "Where're you off to so early, Elada; you go out and about too much, lass, you can't sit still." He didn't even try to hide his posture. Pinyo waved a hand at him but went back home and did not go to the beach on that day, nor on the following days because her father took her to stamp trees on the mountain and she could not say no although the mountain did not attract her as before. When they were done with the work, she was not sure if she'd find David on the beach.

One morning, she mustered her courage and went there. David was sitting on the rock and looking towards St. Anastasia island. Veiled in fog, it looked like an enormous ghostly ship.

"You are not going to Spain on that ship, huh?"

David winced, looked into the girl's eyes and she knew, "You were scared that I could disappear? Forever?" He nodded. "Oh God, David, I'm rushing to you, I'm rushing every minute of the day." And quite unexpectedly, Pinyo started telling him about Hrisoula, about her love with Yorgos and Ovanes and how she loved one with her heart and the other with her soul and how confusing it was because "Aren't they the same, David, heart and soul?"

"They are not," David wrote on the sand.

"And how do you love me?"

The words ran ahead of her. There was no way to take them back, so nothing else remained but to look straight into the young man's eyes. They walked until they reached a small cove sheltered by cliffs from all sides and there David placed his shaking hand on Pinyo's back, and the girl calmed him, "Don't worry about me, I've been ready for a long time, I just had to find you; look how many roads I walked, how many people I met but you were not among them—you, you went as far as Spain and you met so many people, but you came back to this beach so our roads crossed and we came to know each other because, as Hrisoula said, it could happen that people miss each other or meet other people by mistake, but we did not miss each other."

Pinyo pulled down her heavy skirts herself and slipped out of them naked and smooth like a brown chestnut. The first rays of the sun made her skin golden and the wind ruffled the thick bush of her hair. Her small breasts prickled and she stood, her arms limp, and looked at David with her bright eyes without shame or embarrassment; then she lay on the warm sand, closed her eyelids and groped for the silent mouth of the man bent over her, her trembling lips trying to say, "Come to me, David, I know you speak without words." Then they lay on their backs, her head on his shoulder, his dry lips touching her eyelids, and the sky was rocking them.

Pinyo got up and brushed the sand stuck to her body; her nakedness was natural and honest, not only for David, but for the world around, for the sky, the sea, the wind and the rocks so people should know that the world could be made human if it remembered where its umbilical cord was thrown.

They dressed and left. Fishing boats were coming back from the sea, and in the pub up the beach dockers were sitting slurping tripe soup, as always before heading to the quay. When David and Pinyo walked past them, the men grunted and sneered; the girl sensed their glances, greasy like oil, and shuddered. Thank goodness Miron was not here. "Is she that curly everywhere, eh signor?" Pinyo hung on David's hand, "Don't! It doesn't matter," but from the sudden rage and effort, foam appeared in the corners of his lips, and he wiped it with his hand like a child, "It doesn't matter, David, really."

They walked by but Pinyo still felt the porters' looks on her back and feeling anxious, slumped her shoulders.

Old Pinyo kept until her last days the seagull's feather David used to write on the sand *I love you* and other things as they continued to meet on the beach. David lived with the blind artist in a spacious room filled with books to the ceiling. At night he was on the show at the Imperial and during the day he read to oblivion in his room. They were never together in this room: if locked between the four walls, their love would look like an escape or something forbidden; outside, the presence of the sea, its huge breath, its agitation as a gigantic living creature made them feel protected, and the thought that witnesses of their love are the mountainous atmospheres of sky and sea made that love look eternal, like them, "As if nothing bad could happen in this world anymore, huh, David, not only to us two, but in general." Then one morning when Pinyo was especially free in giving herself to her love and her body sang and the wind raised her hair making her look like an olive-skinned rider, something collapsed on the beach. Pinyo winced not being able to stop her headlong gallop through the wild valley of excitement, "It's … stones … falling," she was late in voicing her thought, before she collapsed on the sand herself and felt wind chills clenching her wet belly.

However, it was the dockers, who every morning breakfasted on tripe soup on the beach; they were silently walking the sand towards them. Pinyo grabbed her clothes and darted like a cat to the cliffs pulling on her skirts on the way and screaming, "Run, David, run now, they are many," but David stood there and the dockers closed in on him; he glowered at them with clenched fists, but they sneered, "Calm down, signor, butcher's son, if you keep quiet, nothing bad is going to happen to you; we just want to see if she is as curly everywhere," a short dark one swanked, the gold tooth in his mouth sending a single thin sparkle. David lashed at him and hit his jaw, the docker gasped and spat the gold tooth out; the remaining about ten in the group stopped in their tracks for a second, then pounced upon him, hitting silently. The cove was sheltered and the kicks echoed; Pinyo's terrified screams also echoed off the rocks but the dockers continued to kick and when, exhausted, David collapsed, the short one took a knife and ripped his cheek.

Then Pinyo came running, jumped on the docker's back and clasped her legs around his waist, her fingers poking his eyes. He was yelling and tossing around with Pinyo on his back, and they could barely wrench her off him. She dashed towards David, tried to wipe his face with the wet edge of her skirt and he groaned. "Oh, you're alive," she whispered and opened his fists so the sand he convulsively squeezed ran out. She sat next to him, head on knees, eyes closed. David groaned now and again. Leaning on the rocks around, the dockers were silent. The furthest away was Miron, his hands in the pockets, his legs astraddle.

"Nothing will happen to you if you walk buck naked for us, like Naked Ana, 'Love I am, all of meee,'" the short one grinned again and Pinyo sprang to her feet, "You are crazy, get out right now or I'll call Lefter, the policeman," she threatened but they just laughed, "Love, love with all the dockers …"

Miron raised his hand to order them to shut up; the men obeyed and waited for what he had to say. He approached the girl and clasped one of her wrists in the iron pliers of his fingers, "Your beau, Elada, dumb as a fish, will make nice company for all fish." Pinyo snarled back at him, "Brother Miron, mind your own business! Stay away from us!"

"I was going to ask you to be my wife, Elada. I told you to keep yourself for me, but you showed yourself naked for all the world to see; you can't but keep up with Naked Ana, shame on you now; take off your shirt, naked as a slug, that's how I want to see you …"

"For nothing in the world, Miron, you are crazy!"

"Then I don't care about that dummy over there; he'll either feed the fish, or I'll poke out his eyes so he won't see you ever again."

When he heard this, the shorty brandished the knife right above David's unconscious face. "Don't, no!" Pinyo screamed horrified, "Leave him alone and I'll undress right now; she started pulling off her shirt, her hands shaking, her skirts twisting, the dockers' eyes glossy like olives.

"Don't!" David uttered.

Pinyo stopped as if struck by thunder. She found courage to turn towards David, met his glance and was shaking as he repeated, don't! "God, dear God, it can't be true, it's a miracle!" but she had no time for joy because the shorty was swinging his knife and its edge glinted, so the girl pulled her shirt down her shoulders, let it drop on the sand, stepped out of it and stood before Miron.

The dockers held their breath, their eyes groping her naked body; one sighed loudly. "Walk on the sand to that cliff and back," ordered Miron and Pinyo obeyed. She walked through the sand and her muscles sprang, "Freaks with crooked teeth, slimy slugs," she cursed the dockers many times, but the wind crept up her skin cooling her anger and to her surprise, she found out that it was not only the wind that cooled her hatred but her very anger disappeared on its own; in the end it vanished, melted away, and Pinyo was walking through the water lace freely, without shame or anger, letting the sun caress her, naked like the fish in the sea, like the rocks on the beach, like the water and sky, naked like Naked Ana; those behind her back were dressed, but what did they have in common with the water and the sky, and Ana?

Pinyo came back and bent to pick up her clothes. "You saw what you wanted to see; now, go away!" The shorty grinned, "We want you to ride him in front of us; we couldn't tell from a distance if you were good at it, so show us what a rider you are, or else, your guy will feed the fish for real and nobody will know … because who will they believe, you, a refugee, a nobody, or us, people honest and respectable." The others sneered. In a flash, Pinyo smacked the docker's face. "Hey, look here, the lassie's showing her claws. What if I up and ride you right now, how about it, eh!" The shorty was mad, he caught her waist and squeezed her breasts, she groaned, the man greedily groped her body, "I'll ride you from behind like a filly." He pushed her, face down, against a rock and leaned his body over hers. Then Miron pulled him off the girl and knocked him down on the sand. "Get lost, all of you, hit the road, now!" Reluctantly, the dockers turned back and climbed up the beach.

Miron was watching Pinyo dress.

"You're not dear to me anymore, girl, you should not have done this!"

"Who are you to order my life around?"

"I clipped your wings, winged creature, you won't flitter anymore, you'll never be the same and no man would want to marry you. Your fame will follow you, your naked fame today. And don't blame me for this, just think and you'll see."

Miron left. Pinyo kneeled next to David, who was trying to get up, and put her palm on his forehead.

"The miracle happened, you spoke."

Then Pinyo ran for the artist. Both dragged David home and put ice on the purple swellings on his face and body—the artist kept going down to the basement to fetch new pieces of ice. Dusk was falling when Pinyo went back home. She went to the stables behind the house and took the horse out, hitched it to her father's cart and spurred it on. They rode for a long time. She reached the mountain, stopped in a sparse oak wood, unharnessed, tied the reins to a tree and walked randomly, just needed to walk. She stumbled into thick blackberry bushes, the branches whipped her face, her hair got tangled in the prickly bushes; once she stopped and yelled, "Hrisoulaaa!" The wood answered sympathetically. Reaching a round meadow, she sat under a tree, hugged its trunk and remained there until dark. Curled up at the tree, she suddenly started to howl—it seemed she was howling out of delayed despair and bitterness but she did not know she was howling out of love. She shut up and listened to the silence.

Then the old man appeared. She immediately recognized him: in his beard, a swarm of fireflies; the owl stares from his shoulder as he moves among the trees, and he shines with a ghostly light. It couldn't have been another, it was her old man. "Why were you howling like a beast? It is not appropriate." Pinyo noticed that in the moonlight his eyes were white and lifeless. "Why are your eyes like this, grandpa?" "Because they are turned inside, I see the inside—I was born like that." Pinyo got angry, "Stop staring inside! I know others like you, staring inside—but how about this world, is it a lie? Doesn't this world exist? Why don't you notice it? The artist and David don't either, and many more don't notice it but it is beautiful, this world, only people are good for nothing. Gee, some people do not belong to this whole wide world, but this doesn't make it less beautiful. Why pretend it doesn't exist? Trying to invent another world is like lying to ourselves, but why should we? This world has already been created and what now, leave it to the dockers, eh, grandpa?"

"Smart girl," smiled the old man. Pinyo smiled in turn, "How about you, grandpa, what do you see there, eh?"

"Well, you mentioned it yourself. Another world.

Nobody asks anything there because they know everything."

"You, too, grandpa? Do you know everything? Tell me then, is death really a part of life? Syruie said so in one dream …"

"Why the hurry to know about death?"

She wanted to tell him what had happened to David and her; she had forgotten he knew everything.

"You are impatient, you want a fast answer. People like getting answers. I know what happened to you today and I'll tell you, "Don't think of death, it's not your intrinsic feature. Life is.""

"I'm not asking about myself. They could have killed him today, without batting an eye."

Groaning, the old man sat beside Pinyo. He covered her cold hand with his, sighed, and turning his bottomless eyes toward her, started talking; the girl listened to the echo of his voice, "You ask me if death is a part of life. I could say that life is a part of death, because both are the two halves of the same road. That's what I can tell you for now. Keep walking on your road and don't get distracted. In fact, the road is the destination."

At dawn the fireflies in the old man's beard faded away. The owl was napping, his head buried under his wing. The old man rose groaning and walked straight through the shrubs, melting into the morning half-light.

"Grandpa, will I be able to weep? I want to very much, but I can't!"

She shouted after him though she knew he couldn't hear her.

One of the girl's eyes is smiling, the other, crying. Teardrops like pearls creep down her left cheek, she lets them drip on her shirt, and it's all covered in wet spots. Light dazzles the right side of the face; the light springs from the core of the eye, the core of the girl. The left side is frozen, wet and glossy from the tears. The Fisherwoman wants to half-close one of the eyes, no matter which, "That's not how it is done, child, not at the same time; you won't sense the sweetness of great joy or that of great suffering." She doesn't budge, though, just stands by the cliff waiting to see in which eye the light will fade away first, the smiling or the crying.

At last, the girl half closes her eyes and everything happens simultaneously. The right side of the face fades away, the left dries up. The skin turns pink and the eyelids flutter wearily. The Fisherwoman slaps her forehead, "Don't I know what that is! I just can't name it, but I know what it means when these things happen simultaneously."

She places her hand on Pinyo's shoulder, "You've come here, so you have something to share, and you've already shared it. Without words. And you feel relieved. What else do you need?"

"I want to cry with both eyes, like all the rest of you, but I can't!"

"The rest of us can't do it the way you can."

"I met the old man, the one with the owl. I asked him about things but forgot one vital question—what is happiness, I forgot to ask."

"Why do you need to ask, lassie, you already know everything. Every moment you are not unhappy is happiness."

"There should be something else, Fisherwoman, I know there is. Sometimes it rises from under my ribs, just next to the heart, warms me up and makes me expand, so I can't contain myself. Syruie said that then God is inside us. This must be happiness. But it does not happen all the time—does that mean God is not always in us?"

"It means that we forget about him at times. Completely. Perhaps that's how it should be. Because only when you forget that there's God who watches every step you make, only then could you be completely responsible for all of your life. If it were otherwise, why do we live in this world if we can't take responsibility for our life? I don't say we disavow him, we just forget he watches us and sees everything, so we make mistakes but such is the nature of man ..."

Naked Ana comes along covered with a ragged fishnet, faces Pinyo and smiles with her eyes.

"Fisherwoman, she recognized me!"

"I'm trying to cover her up gradually, to return her to herself, but I should not rush. I could make a mistake. It's a difficult task: dressing Naked Ana is like changing the world. I may not succeed, and winter's coming ..."

Ana reaches out and strokes Pinyo's arm from the shoulder to the fingers; she also strokes the ginger cat and the bread on the table; on the way out, she fondles the white hollyhock at the door of the cabin, runs her fingers on the pores of the rock—she wants to stroke everything, everything in this world, the sun in the daytime, the moon at night, the seagull's feather, the sea sand, the Fisherman's eyes and Pinyo's fingers again, all those; otherwise, why do they exist? Unclad, pitiful, with swampy green eyes and crocus-pale skin, ugly and sad but her smile bright, it hurts to watch her, it hurts to feel her.

Pinyo is crying, with both eyes.

The two continued to meet. They sat on the porch in the artist's house, under the black vine. Fall was coming and they huddled in the collars of their coats—they did not touch at all. Their sanctity and intimacy violated, the bodies started backing away and feeling shamed. At the same time, they were getting attached to each other in another, extraordinary way: somehow, they were painfully growing into each other, becoming one thing. Sometimes when Pinyo was tossing in fever, at the other end of the town, David's body was scorching hot. When David would get one of his rare speaking bouts, Pinyo would run out in the yard and desperately throw up in the weeds.

Sometimes David's mother came by to see him and on occasion, she met Pinyo. The woman sat in the wicker chair, pulled her scarf off her neck and as she was sitting there, she wrapped and unwrapped it around the thin wrist of her hand. Her hair was already showing silver and she was all somehow silver, sunk in sadness she was not aware of. When Pinyo poured linden tea, the cup in the woman's hand shook and she held it with both hands. When she finished her tea, she thanked Pinyo and left. At the door, she looked at Pinyo, smiled only with her eyes, then took David's face between her hands and kissed his forehead. The artist invited her to come again, and she thanked him, "I don't know if I could; Tano, he needs my help. I turn the guts inside out and wash them. It's an easy job and doesn't bother me because I sit on a chair. I have to help this man, I have to." David escorted her down the stairs, and Pinyo waved from above. Zelma was in no hurry to hide round the corner; hanging on her crutches, she stood there looking at the porch as if she'd never been there.

Sometimes as they were sitting together, David would get up and go back to his room, without saying a word. He'd bury himself there in the pile of books and forget Pinyo for quite a while. The girl did not mind. She continued to sit, huddled up in the wicker chair.

"Why is his fate like that, eh?" The artist smiled once, "Fate is neither bad nor good—it's the fate we need. Don't blame him. David feels like this because his male pride was humiliated."

Elada Pinyo burst out in anger, "Why don't I feel humiliated? I don't, though the whole town gossips about me."

The artist moved his face close to hers as if he wanted to peek into her eyes, "What you experienced together by the sea, what you shared together, looked different from a distance. The sight of you at that time stirred the dockers' instincts."

Pinyo blushed to the roots of her hair. The artist let her think about what he'd said, "Except that, you did all that without his permission. You deprived him of the right to have a choice, Pinyo. He told you, don't do it, and you should have listened to him. He asked you with his last remaining strength …"

"They could have killed him and not even bat an eye …"

"They could."

"Oh, God, why are you saying this?"

Pinyo sank in deep thought. David did not leave his room anymore and she went back home.

He dreamt of predator seagulls, like hyenas. They rummaged in the raw animal guts in the butcher's yard, screeched wickedly, whipped wings and dragged in the air brown guts and black spleens. The nightmares of childhood came back, less manageable than ever. He wanted to get out of his dream, tossed, foam spurted from his mouth, but he failed to drive the vision away. Unconsciously, he felt that his oldest nightmare was still sleeping but would wake up soon.

And it came, one midnight: the stone sink, filled with cut lamb's heads, the bitten purple tongues. The white eyes, rolled to the sky. He was also there, with his tongue bitten. Then Elada appeared in her blue skirt; small and scared, she called his name. In vain did he try to tell her something—a tremulous bleating came out of his mouth and joined the chorus. Elada wrung her hands and swung around, about to leave. Don't, he fervently insisted in his mind. She was going away, getting even smaller and more distant and David raised his voice to the sky, don't, unaware that his cry was real.

He woke up drenched in sweat. Thinking about his dream, he decided that it predicted what should happen soon, and that he was the one to make it happen.

On the following morning, he told Elada Pinyo that they needed to separate for a while.

"Do you remember what I told you, lassie, about the leaf and the tree? You sighed when carrying the leaf, but now, I see you've shouldered the tree but you are as silent as a stone. Tell me what's wrong, you might feel relieved. Well, we know everything but should we intervene or not … once the cart is upset, there are many roads to follow, so …"

Then the mother came. She gestured to the old man to leave. She put her hand on Pinyo's shoulder and Pinyo turned around, looked into her mother's eyes and realized that at last, time had started running in her. Pinyo buried her face in her mother's bosom and breathed in love, more, and still more. Her mother rocked her in her lap, rocked her silently for a long time until Pinyo started crying.

She was crying with both her eyes.

On the next day, an international committee arrived in the Kodzhakafali neighborhood to investigate the situation with the refugees from Eastern Thrace. They were French and Pinyo communicated with them in French. They were very surprised. They sat down and asked questions and she told them about Ovanes and Syruie, about Ovanes' telescope and about the books that arrived in Edirne from Marseilles. Old Peter listened agape and was about to burst with pride. The visitors left and two month later, a letter arrived from the French embassy that Elada Petrova's education in France had been arranged.

David was standing behind the velvet curtain and staring into the dawn. Snow had sprayed the narrow street and the yards as if Ferso, the pastry cook, had shaken her flour sacks outside. Her shop across was already lit and you could see her kneading the dough for the morning buns. Her strong hands kneaded the dough lump, twisted it, fondled it, kneaded again. She stopped, tossed a lock of hair off her forehead with one arm and wiped the sweat on her face with her sleeve. She started to shape the buns and arrange them in the baking trays, then took a break by the window, staring aimlessly at her own reflection, her dough-covered hands raised. David almost sensed the smell of vanilla, plum jam and fresh milk.

He stepped out, crossed the street and quietly, so not to scare the young woman, knocked on the window. Ferso raised her head, recognized his face through the sweaty window and smiled. She opened the door, poked his forehead with a doughy finger, settled him in a warm spot and poured hot coffee—its aroma was strong, intoxicating and somehow womanly. Confused, David felt that in her pastry shop Ferso was different. Feeling hot, the woman pressed her cheek to the cool windowpane and laughed,

"Drink your coffee, drink up, or it will get cold!"

David swallowed and burnt his tongue; the pastry cook smiled and continued to roll the buns, arrange them and spread beaten yolks on them. Do you remember the neighborhood by the swamp, my mother and how you dropped by at the same time each morning. The dough was spilling out of the wooden bowl and Ferso was making haste. Her full body looked like the rising dough just before the yeast leavens: the exuberant flesh does not spill but remains tight and female. How did she grow up so fast? He hadn't noticed.

David felt his eyelids were closing. He was sitting half-asleep, melting in the heat. The light snow outside turned into sleet and scratched the windowpane with icy claws. In the oven, the fire blazed wildly in response. Ferso was kneading a new batch of dough. David watched her through his half-closed eyelids: her body sways rhythmically, her breasts push under the apron and when the hair falls over her eyes, she tosses it back with her forearm. She was like warm ginger. The dough in her hands cracked, the bubbles on its surface popped, it smelt of lemon and cinnamon sugar. He wished he could sit like that forever, neither fast asleep nor fully awake. This condition on the boundary of sleep compelled him to perceive his surroundings in a peculiar way. He idly thought that the pastry cook Ferso would never stop kneading her dough. The sleet will turn into rain, the rain into drops of sun, winter into spring, but Ferso will keep on kneading, the dough will rise over the troughs, run through the door to the streets, cool into solid, fragrant drifts, and Ferso will never disappear from life because she is life itself; she will not leave the world because she is the world itself.

He was content to watch this woman and feel that he lacked nothing. In some miraculous way, through her presence, he almost managed to achieve harmony—a moment full and complete. If I know the moment, I've achieved eternity. He made a last effort to think and his head nodded on his chest.

Ferso looked at him, shook her head and continued kneading wearily.

I'm filled up with words to the mouth. Since they can't be spoken, they sometimes scream. I try to speak them without speaking. I gradually calm down and I learn to listen to myself. What my waving hands try to express are only the shadows of the words, not the very words—just like the shadows of the seagulls flying over the sands are not the birds. The words are the other in me. Only when I'm in Ferso's shop, I don't need words. I feel as if I've said everything. The bliss to feel free of speech ... So strange is this feeling, as if bliss itself was speech. It is enough on its own and there's no need to speak.

I'm hiding in Ferso's kingdom, within the scents of vanilla, buns and geranium, in the warmth of her palms on my face, in the tickle of her quick whisper in my ear. A world too female, too imaginary. But this world saves me. I don't need the other world; the world is what we feel as sufficient for us.

The artist drops by sometimes, drinks coffee, eats the

crunchy buns and wonders at Ferso, the colorful spot; "I can see you without seeing you, what kind of woman are you?" he strokes her rounded shoulder and she laughs, "I am all women for you, that's what I am."

The little time I am not with her, I spent locked in my room with the books. The artist and I collected a big library through the years. Sometimes, Ferso reads to him and he keeps repeating to me, "When you have eyes, you have everything. Read my boy and discern. I don't mean you need to accumulate just knowledge; knowledge is not exactly discernment. Discernment is insight, intuition. That's how I understand it. Where can discernment lead man? To God, of course. To the idea of God. However, knowledge is the easy way, from the others' experience, that of the advanced thinkers, of those who discern. It's important you get it on your own; It's not worth it if it's been doled out to you.

I want to object. At the time when Elada read to us, we found among the artist's books old scriptures and John Chrysostom among them. For him, the essential thing for man is faith; it renders meaningless all rational conclusions, not because they are unreasonable, but because being God's design, faith is above them. But I don't want to write just to converse with the artist through Ferso. The thought of Elada makes my heart twinge: once she was the connection between us, a sort of interpreter. She read and the bright cerulean light in her eyes was impossible to look at; her gestures completed her, rounded and caressed my words, which felt extremely alive. Never had I seen or heard speech that was so alive. I can't let Ferso do the same. I wouldn't trust her to speak my words for me.

The artist keeps repeating one thing to me; obviously he's trying to reassure me since he thinks that Elada herself has made the decision to leave me: don't be sad boy, just accept that she's happened to you by chance—see how many years have passed since she left for France but she hasn't written a single letter to you. The chance things we know when they never look back.

I think that if I am to meet again the one and only Elada, I have to look forward; what's in my way is that I can't stop looking back. All in all the artist and I, we don't think the same way, and he thinks that it's a sign that my thinking matures. "You are not getting smarter, you are as smart as you've always been—this is not subject to development. But your thinking has definitely matured into manhood because you think on your own. "Anyway, I've made a choice. While in Ferso's pastry shop, I don't notice how the seasons pass, only winter impresses me: the sleet scratches the window-panes and they sweat from the inside; the wind howls in the chimney and the fire rages; snow suddenly falls and sometimes it seems it has the aroma of plum blossom, shedding down from the heavenly gardens; then the snowdrifts look like piles of frozen, frosty dough. The images that come to me are too pleasing, but I feel this is the way to be done with the nightmares.

It's winter and I know that it is the only season I need. White. Cold outside, warm core inside—only then am I in harmony with myself. I feel protected; the words don't scream in me and don't rush in panic. And here, bliss surges in my chest and rolls into a sweet ball in my belly. This goes on for years until one sudden day I discover that the result will be the same if I buy a paperback notebook and a dozen pencils from the little bookstore on Bogoridi, and start trusting the white sheet with my words.

Up on the goat's path, up there, on one leg, reeling, over the abyss.

Crumbly landslide is the world; it's ugly and I am gasping through my fish mouth.

Swampy, slimy, fiery, hell—the turbid reefs at the bottom moan.

Clods of earth under my feet, I'm falling, only men can fly like this, downwards.

A sudden blade of grass, some tiny stem—and I grab it, my scratched feet digging the earth. Hold on, little blade; hold on, my sorry life, sad and steep, all in swollen wounds,

we two have to creep up, crawl up—we are hell and heaven, we are everything.

Bigger than us is only this little blade of grass, growing in the wild, seemingly by chance.

Farewell from Elada Pinyo's Friend

The last story my old lady told was how David, after speaking his don't, sank into silence again, and how when Pinyo left for France, she got a letter from Ferso, in which her friend described her life with the young man and how calm he was there, with her …

And those four months were over before I could learn the rest. Elada Pinyo gave me her youth, shared her extraordinary fate with me, her full, overflowing life, made my experiences rich, experiences I was deprived of since I had a single love in my life, who quietly died and from whom I had most appropriately separated, dedicating my life to my only son and one–two friends from high school. I did not share Elada Pinyo's story with anybody; I was engrossed in it as if it were my second life, previous or future, and I did not want other people peeking in. But after some reflection, I realized that if I told it in a book, more people would become rich like me, would stir up the swamp of their stagnant life, would want something to happen, and once we strongly want it, it can really happen.

I sat down and quite unawares wrote what the kind reader, having reached my last lines, has surely already read.

However, I felt like giving this story a certain end, though putative, so I dared a modest co-authorship with Elada Pinyo and, ultimately, her fate. Anyone could accept or reject this afterword or create another that would best match this extraordinary plot.

The door of the shop opened and Pinyo appeared on the threshold.

"Come," she said, "let's go. You can't live like that. I mean, you cannot not live, like that."

"Elada."

Without any effort as if he hadn't been silent for years, David spoke. At last, he wanted to speak. Pinyo closed her eyes tight and opened them after a whole century, "Now, you see it's possible. Everything in this world is possible if you want it to happen. Speak, David, come out and come to the world, David, live, David, be happy and be sad, be both at the same time. I'm sure it's possible: if you are happy, it's even impossible not to be sad. That's how real happiness is, what do you say? Speak, David, you found your words, tell us what happiness is! I can't wait to hear it from your mouth! Is Ferso your happiness or I am that thing, just go ahead, speak. It could be neither of us, tell us, we want to hear, David."

"I think … I think that the art of happiness is to make life give you more than is seemingly possible." That's what David said. "Wow, that was a long speech," Pinyo claps her hands, as much Elada now as she is Pinyo because he called her so; she did not grasp the meaning of what David said, but she does not need to understand any meaning now because she knows everything as it is, without words. Both David and she learn the same things in different ways: everything is complex with him, much thought over; with her, it's simple and happens on its own.

"Come on, David, say forgive me to Ferso. You forgive me too, lass."

Ferso, a green-eyed willow, watches and doesn't move. The dough in her hands flows over to the floor and runs like a river. "Forgive me, Ferso, I am everything to this man, every day in his life. You, Ferso, were his shelter, his mother's womb, his warm hollow, but wind does not reach it, rain does not fall and storms don't howl here—this man does not need a shelter. I know what he needs; I know that better than he does: I am his wind and rain, his thunder and lightning, Ferso, so farewell, my friend."

Together, they come out to the street, a thin stream of Ferso's dough follows into their footsteps, draws some signs, something secret, soft and mysterious. But Elada Pinyo leads David and he knows this is the way. "I am leading you now but later, your turn will come; we'll take turns in life, David, when you learn how to walk firmly on your path."

They walk for a long time and at last reach the Fisherwoman's steep top. They creep up together, side by side. The woman up there is waiting for them, motionless.

"Fisherwoman, David said *Elada!*"

Here comes Naked Ana, shy as a child, dressed in a sleeveless hemp shirt. The Fisherwoman shrugs her shoulders, "I did not want to do this, but it's winter. She got used to my clothes but more importantly, she is still Naked Ana. Look into her the eyes and you'll understand what I am talking about."

"Fisherwoman, did you hear? David said *Elada*. He spoke."

"It's fate, my girl."

"Gee, if I hadn't rushed to the pastry shop the moment

I came back from Marseilles, right from the ship, fate would not have moved her little finger."

"You are fate, Elada. Nobody has escaped from it and David won't either. Didn't I tell you I come up with stories and tell them to myself? I promised David when he was little and climbed up the slope to me for the first time, I promised to tell him one of those stories—well, I'll try to come up with another story now, just for you two."

They all sit. Ana strokes David's fingers. The Fisherwoman feels the Karakachan ring on Elada Pinyo's pinkie. "Look at that little ring, Pinyo, and imagine that a thief steals it from you as you are walking on Bogoridi. A policeman rushes after him, but the thief puts it in his mouth, swallows it and quickly disappears. What happens to the ring? It's clear, the thief will go back home, will squat in his yard and push hard once or twice and then … you know. But, no luck, Elada, a hen will quickly spot the ring and thinking it a grain of corn, peck and swallow it. What will the thief do then? He'll be fast to chase the hen, place it on a log of wood, cut its head and gut it as much as he can. But no luck again, Elada. A vulture will hover above, swoop down greedily, grab the gut with the ring in its beak and drag it for a long time; it will hover long above the lake looking for a place to perch and drop the ring flush in the water. In the water, as you have already guessed, a fish will swallow it. What else remains to happen to your little gold ring? You often stay with old Peter on the beach with a fishing rod like a man, so you'll catch a carp with your hook and if you are destined to wear that ring, it'll be that very carp with the ring in its belly."

"So, you rushed into the pastry shop, Elada, to claim

your David and he chose to leave with you. Why do you think he did it? Another girl was there, a real pearl, how is she inferior? Why can't she hold a candle to you? But David got up and left because that's what he wanted and because that's what's written in the stars—up there in the stars, boy, it's scribbled. That was my tale about fate, but you can think of a better one if you can, I don't mind."

"Gee, Fisherwoman, it was a great story. Thank you for it!"

David smiles. Ana puts her head on Elada Pinyo's lap and falls asleep. "Let her sleep; she's tired and needs some rest." "Naked Ana is very tired, David," the girl whispers and strokes Ana's fingers. Ana smiles in her sleep. "She has not forgotten, no, she hasn't forgotten to smile! You don't know what Naked Ana is—she is everything we can't do without, but I can't explain that very well. Since I looked into her eyes, I started to guess the meaning, David, because I know about everything inside me, but only the meaning escapes me. I've started to guess it only recently, since I met Ana. I need to know time; time is something I don't understand either. Do you know about these things, David, time and meaning, do you?"

"I know … what you are … Elada …"

Elada Pinyo dazzles the man with the blue in her eyes. She touches his hand, whispers and often repeats his name.

The Fisherwoman shakes her head, gets up groaning and heads down the slope.